BOM-CRIOULO

ADOLFO CAMINHA

BOM-CRIOULO

The Black Man and the Cabin Boy

by
Adolfo Caminha

Translated from Portuguese
by
E. A. Lacey

Gay Sunshine Press
San Francisco

Publication of this book made possible in part by a grant from the National Endowment for the Arts, Washington, D.C.

Cover drawing by José Lima (Brazil)
Cover design by Speros Bairaktaris
Layout by Timothy Lewis
Typeset by Xanadu Graphics, Inc., Cambridge, Mass.

Footnotes have been prepared especially for this edition by E. A. Lacey and Raul de Sá Barbosa.

Library of Congress catalog card number: 82-11796

ISBN: 0-917342-87-9 (cloth)
ISBN: 0-917342-88-7 (paper)

Gay Sunshine Press
PO Box 40397
San Francisco, CA 94140
Illustrated catalog of titles available on request.

INTRODUCTION
by
Raul de Sá Barbosa

In Brazil, if one says simply "Machado", everybody knows one means Joaquim Maria Machado de Assis (1839-1908), the author of *Memórias póstumas de Brás Cubas,* familiar to Americans as *Epitaph of a small winner* since the 1952 William S. Grossman translation. But if one says "Caminha", the ordinary reader is thrown back four centuries and thinks automatically of Pedro Vaz de Caminha (1450-1500), Portuguese navigator and chronicler of Cabral's fleet, who wrote for the king's information and posterity's delight the official account of the admiral's discovery. Adolfo Caminha, the 19th century Brazilian writer, is just "the other Caminha", not irrelevant, not unknown, but largely and deliberately ignored, eighty five years after his death.

He had started as a poet and ended up a novelist, and a Naturalist novelist at that. A rather late Naturalist, because literary movements occur in Brazil with considerable delay. Romanticism, first in poetry, then in prose, did not begin before 1830, Realism, not before 1870; Naturalism, not before 1880. Of these schools, none so natural an outlet for the Brazilian soul as Romanticism, none so appropriate an instrument of national expression. Self-absorbed, impetuous, lyrical, the Brazilians took to Romanticism as fish take to water, and were never the same again. Later literary movements had, all of them, a Romantic touch, present even in the somber world of Caminha's novels. But his social awareness, his sexual frankness, his ready acceptance of the bad along with the good, his wholehearted adoption of unconventional human behaviour turned opinion against him. Brazil was very backward in his time.

Handicapped by poverty, by disease, by his own temperament, by hostility in his milieu, he led a hand-to-mouth existence, brightened only by his love for wife and daughters. Too young and daring to be accepted, too brilliant to be forgiven, he soon burned out. Born in 1867, he died in 1897, before completing 30 years of age and after a meteoric career. His genius had antagonized virtually everyone who mattered, and his work — polemic, provocative, misunderstood — fell into an abyss of silence. There was no vilification in the press, no orchestrated chorus of calumny. But both the Establishment and the literary coteries (like the *Padaria Espiritual* in his native Ceará) ignored his work as soon as consumption had rid them of him. His masterpiece, *Bom-Crioulo* published in 1895, had four editions in seventy years; and the second one is so inaccurate that it should not be counted as one. (The last two editions appeared in 1956 and 1966.)

Agripino Grieco, with his infallible flair, does him justice in *Evolução da prosa brasileira* (1933; *Evolution of Brazilian Prose*), saying that Caminha was "sarcastic even when half pious", pointing to the excellence and originality of his talent and of his books — "novels that are not a mere semblance of Naturalism...[or a product] of a simple parasite who sat at Zola's table..." He continues: "Because [Caminha] detested easy literature, this man who knew how to see with such acumen human mediocrity deserves to have his books reissued."

Well, this is now being done. In spite of having been removed from the cheap-priced series of Brazilian classics known as Edições de Ouro (Golden Editions), Caminha begins to receive his due ("He used to be one of our authors but, alas, not anymore", somebody was told by the Golden Editions people not long ago when in search of a copy of *Bom-Crioulo*). In 1980, a television station in São Paulo dramatized and showed, in four chapters, one of his short stories, and an unpublished one at that. Editora Três is advertising a paperback edition of *The Schoolgirl*, to be sold at newspaper stands. Editora Nova Fronteira is contemplating the publication of the complete works, including texts never printed before and presently under the guard of Sr. Mauricio Caminha de Lacerda, the worthy grandson of the novelist. The material includes: an early play; a complete novel, *Angelo*, set in the XVIIth century; an unfinished one, *The Emigré*, about the 1877 drought, which cost the life of the novelist's mother; an autobiographical sketch, covering the first period of his life (from birth to definite transfer to Rio de Janeiro); assorted poetry (poetry was not Caminha's strong point); correspondence with literary friends; a preface to the collected poems of Alves Lima, a bard from Ceará; a handful of translations from Balzac (one of his cherished dreams was to see the whole of Balzac in Portuguese).

6

Adolfo Ferreira Caminha was born in Aracati, Ceará, then a northeast province of the Empire of Brazil, on May 29, 1867. His father was Raimundo Ferreira dos Santos Caminha; his mother, Maria Ferreira Caminha, died when he was only 9 years old. His uncle Alvaro took him and his brother Abdon to his house and brought them up. (Abdon, who was also a navy officer, committed suicide in 1912.)

Adolfo attended public school and in 1883 entered the naval school (Escola de Marinha), at Ilha das Enxadas (Hoes Island), Guanabara Bay. Like Bonaparte in Brienne, he was from the beginning a solitary figure, shying away from the company of his classmates, and taking refuge in books. Aloof, reticent, averse to practical jokes, inimical to sport, to muscle bouts, to nakedness in the *palestra*, he passed his time reading, studying and already writing, more often than not under a big tamarind tree. There functioned, *al fresco*, the offices of the student's literary society, the Phenix.

In 1885, the Phenix promoted a meeting to honour the memory of Victor Hugo. The great man had just died. The emperor himself was present, and Caminha spoke for the students. And instead of praising in Hugo the poet or the novelist, he glorified the republican. It was a scandal. Only Pedro II stayed unaffected. "Don't punish the boy," he told the admiral-director, "it is no serious matter. A poet's fantasies..."

One year later, a midshipman on board the brand-new battleship *Almirante Barroso*, Caminha went to the United States in the course of an instruction cruise. The ship went first to New Orleans, for the international exhibition. In spite of the efforts of the Brazilian consul, Salvador de Mendonça, a distinguished writer and journalist, "the anachronistic Empire of His Lordship D. Pedro II", as Caminha said on the occasion, was poorly represented. The ship, though, was an instant success and saved the day.

Caminha took rooms at the Saint Charles Hotel, and it is easy to imagine him looking at the beautiful street from his window on the second floor, having a luxurious bath "in a marble bathtub", eating oysters for lunch (washed down by a bottle of Sauterne) and then chewing a cigar ("chewing is the term, because I am not too fond of cigars..."). After the meal, Baedecker in hand, and very trim in his uniform, he went for a stroll down Canal Street, through Bourbon Street and the Vieux Carré (that gayest of places), to the French Market.

He toured the country, although not extensively. But he saw New York; Niagara Falls; Washington D.C. (Cleveland was president, "a nice specimen of yankee: corpulent, hair combed back, resolute stare, thick moustache. . ."); Baltimore; Philadelphia, "with its matchless zoo"; Annapolis, at the time "a sort of African quilombo"; West Point; Newport.

The rich store of images brought back from the trip inspired *No país dos ianques* (1894; *In Yankee Land*), published in installments by the Fortaleza paper *O Norte*, under the title "Notas de viagem" before being put in book form. Caminha was a gifted observer, and the book is a sharply critical comment on the so-called 'American way of life', its mechanization and commercialization.

Back in Ceará, as second lieutenant (1887), he frequented the literary circles and contributed to the local newspapers. Suddenly, an insane love for a young woman of the best society, Isabel Jataí de Barros, upset the apple cart. She was only 16 but married to an uncle who happened to be an army officer. The lady deserted her husband to join him. Caminha was threatened, then ostracized and finally recalled to Rio de Janeiro by the last navy minister of the monarchy. Surprisingly, the man understood him and sent him back, unpunished. But then the government fell; and with the government, the regime. Caminha was summoned again. This time he had to forsake the navy. His discharge was discreet. The Ministry gave him a month's sick leave and only then formalized his resignation.

This spelled financial ruin. Thanks to Rui Barbosa, the new Minister of Finance, the former officer secured a clerkship in the civil service, and from then on supported himself and his family doing secretarial work and writing articles for the press. He was remarkably devoted and loyal to his wife and daughters (Aglaís and Belkiss), but the next years were the darkest of his life. They lived modestly, first in Fortaleza, then in Rio (at Visconde de Itaúna Street 261-B, facing the gas factory). His eldest daughter, Belkiss, afflicted with a congenital bronchial condition, died of tuberculosis (as her father would too) when only four months old. There was little money: the editors refused unsolicited originals, the published books did not sell. Everything conspired to aggravate the general if muffled animosity against him.

Caminha had been, in Ceará, one of the founders of the literary circle *Padaria Espiritual* (Spiritual Bakery), whose headquarters were called The Oven, and whose paper was inevitably named *Bread*. In Fortaleza, as in Rio, he dabbled in literary criticism, making more enemies than impact with his reviews. He founded a magazine, *A Nova Revista*, and worked for important newspapers, like *A Gazeta de Notícias*. *Cartas literárias* (1895; *Literary Correspondence*) is a compilation of his articles on literature. According to Alfredo Bosi, *História concisa da literatura brasileira* (1970), his criticism was inspired by Taine but open to the Symbolism of Cruz e Sousa. It amply attests to his insight and independence. He used to sign off "C.A.", and for a time his "letters" were attributed to Constâncio Alves or to Capistrano de Abreu. *O País*, a leading newspaper, then under the direction of the great republican leader Quintino Bocaiuva, first Minister of Foreign Affairs of the Provisional Government, was proud of him and chose *In Yankee Land* as a Christmas gift for its subscribers.

A last — and minor — novel, *A Tentação* (*Temptation*) was published posthumously.

The writer died on January 1, 1897. A subscription held among friends yielded sixty mil réis. He was buried in St. John the Baptist cemetery (grave 3993). With the family away for the ceremony, thieves ransacked the poor house on Rua Visconde de Itaúna, taking the little that was worth pilfering.

***

Caminha admired Balzac, but not with servility. From the European Naturalists he took the belief in fate and doom and the taste for the scabrous. "Even his occasional bad taste," says Lúcia Miguel Pereira, "makes more convincing the sad condition of man he evokes..."

He owes much to Zola and more still to Eça de Queirós, the Portuguese author of *O Crime do Padre Amaro* (1875; *Father Amaro's Crime*) and *O Primo Basílio* (1878; *Cousin Basílio*). Eça and the Brazilian *chef d'école* Aluísio Azevedo — *O Mulato* (1881; *The Mestizo*), *Casa de pensão* (1884; *Boardinghouse*) and *O Cortiço* (1890; *Tenement*) — are his closest models. One of his main characters, the student Zuza, who loves Maria do Carmo, the schoolgirl, reads Aluísio. *Casa de pensão* is his favorite book, an *important* book, he used to brag.

Caminha's novel *A Normalista* draws on a real story of a young girl seduced by her foster father, a certain João Maciel da Mata Gadelha, known as João da Mata. Their son, stillborn, is buried secretly in the country. And in the country the girl finds someone else to marry. Surprisingly, a happy ending.

"If *A Normalista* is an immoral book" — wrote Caminha, exasperated — "what about the novels by Aluísio Azevedo? Are they to be proscribed from the public libraries? In this case, what to do with *A Carne* (*Flesh*), by Júlio Ribeiro? Shouldn't it be burned ceremoniously in an *auto-da-fé*? Isn't it the same question that sent *Madame Bovary* to the tribunals? *Madame Bovary*, that 'code of the new art' as Zola has said...*A Normalista*, I repeat, is a sincere book, the fruit of hard work, and a thousand times better than the useless bosh that our papers publish every day."

In Caminha's work society and navy are only stereotypes. Gastão Penalva understood it very well. In his *Maritime History of Brazil* (1939) he wrote: "The navy of *Bom-Crioulo*, the scenery in which the novel takes place, the facts and characters that animate the plot are not real, are not places and people he knew... The hero and the episodes are based in more ancient times, tragic and adventurous times, when the pirates lived, when ships cruised for months, and there was only sky and water... What influenced him were literary reminiscences, exploits of other lands and peoples, and the fallacious oral tradition, which ruins history and misinterprets myths."

The young cabin-boy himself, the blond sailor Aleixo, with whom both the negro Amaro and the Portuguese woman Carolina fall in love, is another stereotype: the sempiternal *ephebus*, sung by Greeks (Theocritus) and Romans (Virgil) alike. The name "Aleixo" is a transparent clue.[1]

"Amaro" is another one. According to Antenor Nascentes, *Dicionário etimológico da língua portuguesa* (1952), Amaro comes from the Lat. *Maurus*, a Moor or black. The word can also be interpreted as 'bitter', from the Lat. *amarus*. Caminha may have thought of both things when choosing the name. (He may also have been thinking of the verb "amor", "to love", and of the Moor of Venice, Othello — tr.) Bom-Crioulo, the name by which Amaro was known, is best translated in English as the Good Black Man.

---

[1] From the greek *Alexis*, lat. *Alexius*.
"Pastor Corydon ardebat/*Alexim*, delicias domini..." ("The shepherd Corydon with love was fired for fair Alexis, his own master's joy..."). Virgil, "Eclogue" II, 1-2.

ADOLFO CAMINHA'S
BOM-CRIOULO
by
Robert Howes

Adolfo Caminha's *Bom-Crioulo* is a remarkable novel. Published in Rio de Janeiro in 1895, the year of the Oscar Wilde trials in England, it deals in an open and straightforward way with a homosexual love affair between two Brazilian sailors. It is remarkable because the main character is black, a former slave, when black slavery in Brazil had only been finally abolished seven years earlier. It is remarkable also because of the skill with which the author evokes the emotions and thought processes of his uneducated, illiterate hero, looking forward to Graciliano Ramos's masterpiece *Vidas secas (Dry Lives)*. But above all the novel stands out because of the way in which the homosexual nature of the hero's love is accepted as natural, with no attempt at moralizing or explanation. For this reason *Bom-Crioulo* can bridge the years and appeal strongly to the modern reader.

The novel tells the story of a black runaway slave who enlists as a sailor on a Brazilian warship and falls in love with a young white cabin-boy. It is told in a sober and economical fashion with events progressing steadily towards the dramatic climax. As this approaches Bom-Crioulo takes on the stature of a tragic hero. The ending of the novel is not the stereotypic punishment reserved for The Homosexual but rather the inevitable outcome of a Great Passion.

Brazilian critics have long held an ambivalent attitude towards the novel. They admire Caminha's skill as a writer, particularly his brilliant descriptions of everyday life on board ship and in Rio, while deploring his choice of homosexuality as a subject and his forthright descriptions of sexual matters. What shocks the critics most is the author's failure to be shocked by the events he describes. Adolfo Caminha openly describes

11

scenes of masturbation and wet dreams, and leaves us in no doubt that Bom-Crioulo is the active partner and Aleixo the passive one in their sexual relations. He accepts the homosexual nature of their relationship and describes it with the same respect usually accorded to heterosexual love, as when he describes Bom-Crioulo's falling in love with Aleixo (see pages 44-45).

The events of Caminha's life provide a key to an understanding of the novel. Caminha was embarked on a promising career as a naval officer serving in the northern city of Fortaleza when he began an affair with the wife of an army lieutenant. Eventually she left her husband and went to live openly with Caminha. The scandal was immense, involving as it did the rivalry between the two branches of the Armed Forces. It went to the highest political levels in Rio where Caminha was forced to choose between his career and the woman. He chose to resign from the Navy. The couple were driven out of Fortaleza by social ostracism and moved to Rio where they lived in obscurity. Caminha contracted tuberculosis and died at the age of 29.

Caminha published two main novels, both of which reflect the events described above. The first, A normalista (The trainee teacher), which was published in 1893 and told the story of a girl in Fortaleza who was seduced and made pregnant by her guardian, was based on a scandal which had actually taken place some years earlier. The tone of the novel is not particularly bitter but the satirical portraits of some of the characters were clearly meant as an attack on real people in the city which had ostracized him. The novel gives an engaging picture of everyday life in late nineteenth century Fortaleza, with its inhabitants given over to illicit love affairs, nosiness, gossip and hypocrisy. These are viewed as the normal state of affairs, so when the unfortunate heroine goes off quietly to have her baby and it dies at birth, this is seen as a happy release and opens the way for her to make a good marriage. Ultimately the message is that the way of life of Fortaleza's citizens is too mediocre and hypocritical to be worthy of any moral consideration.

Similarly, underlying Bom-Crioulo is criticism of the Brazilian Navy, which was also partly responsible for the wreck of Caminha's career and his personal problems. This is clearly seen in the descriptions of two brutal floggings given to Bom-Crioulo as a punishment under the Navy's code of discipline. As a young cadet Caminha had published a courageous article attacking the use of the lash. His treatment of homosexuality must also be regarded in a similar light. For example, he refers snidely to an officer who was well known to take a very personal interest in his men (no doubt the real identity of this character could readily have been guessed by contemporaries). Furthermore the way in which Bom-Crioulo's affair with Aleixo is accepted with little more than a knowing smile by his officers and fellow sailors implies that this was a common event on warships, a damning allegation in the eyes of the Navy which even in the 1930s apparently made an attempt to stop the book being distributed.[1] *Bom-Crioulo*, then, aims to shock by accepting as normal a state of affairs which "right-thinking" people would expect not to be treated as normal.

At this point it is worth considering what Caminha's views on homosexuality were. The late nineteenth century was a period when the traditional religious view of sodomy as a sin was being superseded, at least in more progressive circles, by what has been termed the "medical model" of homosexuality as a sickness. This was part of a general growth of interest in science and medicine, and was reflected in literature by the development of Naturalism, of which Emile Zola was the leading exponent. Naturalism was "an attempt to apply to literature the discoveries and methods of nineteenth-century science. . . . To the Naturalists man is an animal whose course is determined by his heredity, by the effect of his environment and by the pressures of the moment" (Furst & Skrine, *Naturalism*, London, 1971).

Adolfo Caminha is often numbered among the Brazilian Naturalists largely because of his choice of "scabrous" subjects such as homosexuality and his unvarnished treatment of all sexual matters. If we compare *Bom-Crioulo* with a slightly earlier Portuguese novel which unashamedly followed the tenets of the Naturalist school, we can better see how far Naturalism influenced Caminha's view of homosexuality.

Abel Botelho's *O Barão de Lavos* (*Baron Lavos*) was published in Oporto, Portugal in 1891 and is one of the earliest novels in which the main character is clearly identified as a homosexual and whose plot revolves around his homosexuality. Caminha was accused of plagiarizing Botelho for *Bom-Crioulo*. Although Caminha knew Botelho's work, virtually the only factor which both novels have in common is their protagonists' homosexuality.

Underneath Botelho's scientific and medical language there is a certain prurient fascination with the subject (together with

---

[1] Braga Montenegro. "Adolfo Caminha", *Clã* (Fortaleza), 8 (17) Junho 1958, pp. 96-100.

some interesting descriptions of gay cruising in nineteenth century Lisbon). The overwhelming tone of the novel, however, is negative and hostile towards homosexuality. This contrasts with Adolfo Caminha's approach, for example in the passage in which Bom-Crioulo attempts to come to terms with his feelings for Aleixo after the boy has yielded to him. In simple language Caminha recreates the thoughts of an uneducated man. To Bom-Crioulo homosexuality is something natural which cannot be explained but must be accepted.

This is not to say that Caminha himself was unaware of contemporary medical theories. In the course of the novel he uses the word "uranista" (a term coined by German writers on homosexuality) and refers to masturbation as a practice which doctors condemn (a reference to the contemporary theory of masturbatory insanity). Later Caminha defended his novel against attacks by the critics in an article in which he showed at least a passing knowledge of the main scientific writers on homosexuality:

After all, what is Bom-Crioulo? *Nothing more than a case of sexual inversion as studied in Krafft-Ebing, Moll, Tardieu and the books on forensic medicine!*[1]

Little of this knowledge appears directly in the novel, however, and science's loss is literature's gain. Caminha's descriptions of homosexual behavior seem to be drawn from personal observation rather than from medical textbooks. Having served on several ships and made a long voyage to the United States in 1886, he was no doubt aware of what went on "in the Navy" and all his books show a worldly-wise attitude towards sex. Naturalism gave him the license to write about subjects such as homosexuality but it did not directly influence the way he developed his novel.

In the same article Caminha went on to say:

Which is more pernicious: Bom-Crioulo, *in which homosexuality is studied and condemned, or those pages which are in circulation preaching in a philosophical tone the break-up of the family, concubinage, free love and all sorts of social morality?*

---

[1] Adolfo Caminha "Um livro condenado." *Nova revista*, no. 2 (1896), quoted in Saboia Ribeiro, *Roteiro de Adolfo Caminha* (1964), pp. 59-60.

Homosexuality can be said to be "condemned" in the use of expressions such as "crime against nature" to describe Bom-Crioulo's sodomizing of Aleixo, or in the novel's conclusion. However, taking the book as a whole, homosexual love comes N.B. off better than its heterosexual counterpart. Contrast the restrained dignity and seriousness of the pages in which Caminha describes Bom-Crioulo's growing involvement with Aleixo and his final conquest of him with the superbly comic and grotesque scene in which Miz Carolina drags the boy into bed with her; or Bom-Crioulo's tormented despair at Aleixo's abandonment of him with the light assertion that neither Miz Carolina nor Aleixo would have continued their affair if the butcher who kept her had stopped paying the rent for her house.

Caminha's attitude towards homosexuality was therefore ambivalent. But his own experience after breaking the rules of the sexual code no doubt reinforced the liberal and humane outlook which he had displayed in championing the abolition of slavery and flogging, making him responsive to other life styles which defied the social conventions.

The most important demonstration of this responsiveness appears in Caminha's portrayal of Bom-Crioulo and his refusal to stereotype him. Bom-Crioulo is a character in the round, far removed from the conventional image of the Homosexual. This stereotype already existed in Brazilian literature, examples from Aluísio Azevedo's novel *O cortiço* of 1890 being Botelho, the "dirty old man" who touches up a student; Albino, an effeminate young man who spends most of his life among the washerwomen; and the predatory lesbian prostitute Léonie. A more fully developed example from Portugal was Abel Botelho's degenerate, artistically-inclined aristocrat in *O Barão de Lavos*, a novel mentioned earlier.

Bom-Crioulo, on the other hand, is a huge muscular black, a run-away slave who enlists as a seaman and who imposes respect on his fellow sailors and officers by his physical strength and courage. Violent and dangerous when drunk, hard-working and disciplined when sober, he is capable of acts of bravery and kindness, such as rescuing Miz Carolina from her attackers or carrying an epileptic to hospital. In short he is a credible ✓ character who engages the interest and sympathy of the reader. The development of his passion for the cabin-boy further serves to round out the character. Bom-Crioulo's original interest in Aleixo turns into raging desire and infatuation which develops into quiet affection as they live together. Later, as he realizes he has been abandoned by the boy, love is mixed with jealousy,

15

hatred and increasing despair which Caminha skilfully describes as they lead toward the fatal climax.

The character of Bom-Crioulo gives the novel grandeur and stops it from becoming a sociological tract. Caminha allows the novel to develop according to its own logic. The author accepts his protagonist's homosexuality as part of life's rich fabric and so Bom-Crioulo grows into a powerful, living character, one of Brazilian literature's tragic heroes.

TRANSLATOR'S PREFACE
by
E. A. Lacey

The translation of this grim and profoundly subversive novel from a long-forgotten past and a distant country has been a useful historical and intellectual exercise for the translator, and I hope a perusal of the text may be equally useful to the reader. A book like *Bom-Crioulo* truly deserves to be better known in the arena of world literature, both for the fortuitous fact of its being the world's first modern gay novel and for the sad, shocking verities about the human condition presented in its lucid, imperturbable, almost complacent *exposé* of life in the Brazilian navy and in the *bas-fonds* of the city of Rio de Janeiro some one hundred years ago. Though the novel is short, and relatively simple in both plot and language, it did produce certain problems in translation that are worth a brief mention.

To begin with, the nautical vocabulary employed in the descriptions of life on the corvette and of harbour and naval activities in the port of Rio de Janeiro is both technical and quite archaic. I have tried to familiarize myself as much as possible with the construction and operation of nineteenth-century ships, but inevitably the modern English equivalents found will on occasion lack precision. I trust readers more versed in the subject will charitably forgive my lack of expertise and make their own corrections.

As Mr. Sá Barbosa has noted in his Introduction, Brazilian Naturalism is both Romantic and Naturalistic at the same time, and Caminha was definitely a Romantic Naturalist. As such, he shares certain characteristics with both schools. One of his Romantic inheritances, for example, is a distinct fondness for "set pieces" of description or narration. These, while they are sometimes masterpieces of vigour, economy and significant detail — for example, the unforgettable scene of the canings in Chapter I, or the description of the sailors singing and playing the guitar, and later sleeping, in Chapter III — on other occasions do not particularly advance the action of the novel (for example, the long digression on the past of Miz Carolina, in Chapter IV). Often they seem to have been inserted in obedience to some caprice of the author (like the carillon playing *Les cloches de Corneville* in Chapter VII), or are rather frigidly conventional and only of limited interest, such as the description of the storm, in Chapter III, or the many descriptions, *passim*, of harbour activities and of the general landscape of Rio de Janeiro. There was a strong temptation to excise such passages, but in view of the novel's historical interest they were retained. However, a description such as "above, in the dome of the great half-sphere of the sky, ablaze with noonday light, the blue, always the clear blue, the pure blue, the sweet, transparent, infinite, mysterious blue", even with its reminiscence of Machado de Assis, cannot be considered one of the great passages of Romantic literature — and there are too many such in *Bom-Crioulo*.

One of Caminha's pronouncedly Naturalistic characteristics, on the other hand, inherited from writers like Zola and Eça de Queirós (and shared with authors like Hardy and Conrad, whom Caminha, for chronological and cultural reasons, cannot have read, though the affinity with Conrad is striking, both in vocabulary and style, and in the choice of subject matter), is the excessive use of a rather dry, technical, scientific, often anatomo-medical vocabulary, especially in dealing with human physiological and psychic phenomena, which seems incredibly *un*Romantic and unfeeling to the modern reader. Words like prognathism, hermaphroditism, dyspneia, ecchymosis, strabismus, callipygian and other less objectionable terms, such as pathological, magnetic, galvanic and genetic, litter the text. Such terminology, for the Naturalistic author, served both for exactitude and as euphemism, as, for example, when masturbation is called "an ugly and depressing but very human act" or "excesses which doctors condemn", anal intercourse becomes "the act against nature", and semen is "prolific gum" or "the generative juice of man".

Yet an attempt was made to respect Caminha's euphemisms, which may seem ridiculous and unnecessary today, but which, like "limbs" for "legs", reflect the man, the style and the period. With direct reference to Bom-Crioulo's homosexuality (and I do not wish to be drawn into a discussion of whether Caminha was or was not gay — there is evidence in both directions, and it is conflicting — except to note that a career in the navy is certainly among the most likely to have familiarised him with homosexual activity, and growing up and living in a traditionally sexually relaxed country such as Brazil would tend to have made him tolerant of it: what is important to note, however, is that he was a Naturalist — or polymorphously perverse, as we might say today — to whom by definition any and all human phenomena were "natural" and "right"), the author four times uses the term "pederasta" (always more acceptable in Portuguese, under the influence of French "pédé", than in English), once "uranista" and various times euphemisms, such as "Greek love", "Greek carnality", "Priapus", etc. It was felt that "pederast" was too derogatory in English to be used, and "uranist" too dated, so substitutes had to be found. Since "homosexual" was not a very common word at that time, I tried to restrict its use as much as possible. Similarly, Miz Carolina's sexual inclinations, which might at a later date have been labelled bisexual or lesbian (she liked feminine-looking boys) have been called here by the name given them in the text — "hermaphroditic tendencies".

With regard to obscenities and profanities, the only ones which Bom-Crioulo employs in speech, besides the mild "que diabo!" ("what the devil! what the hell!") are, once only, "merda" ("shit"), and, quite frequently, the popular expression, "puta que o(s) pariu" ("son-of-a-bitch, sons of bitches"), which Caminha always chastely abbreviates, omitting the offensive word "puta" ("whore"). This is not necessarily a sign of Caminha's hypocrisy or caution. The Portuguese language, in both its Brazilian and its Portuguese variant, is, in keeping with the mild, tolerant character of Brazilians and Portuguese, considerably less obscene, profane and scatological than English or, for example, Spanish. Few indeed are the popular expressions of this nature used in daily speech to express annoyance or anger.

With regard to more generalised use of slang terms, there was no attempt to render this translation in strict nineteenth-century style, but a general appropriateness of vocabulary was sought. Thus, Bom-Crioulo is allowed to call the cabin-boy "kid" in speech, but in the descriptive and narrative passages he is always referred to as "boy" or "lad". Similarly, the offensive term "nigger" was used when, in direct speech, there was obviously the desire to insult or give offense, but Portuguese "negro" and "crioulo" are always translated "black (man)" or "Negro" in other contexts.

Finally, it may be remarked that Caminha shares the generally mechanistic, determinist, decidedly pessimistic bias of the other Naturalists of his school and time (despite positivist currents that dominated socio-political thinking in Brazil in that era). This is perhaps as much due to the unhappy circumstances of his life and to his familiarity with Brazilian reality, then as now, as to any literary or philosophical doctrine. At all events, to him human beings are evidently mere animals — animal metaphors so abound in the text as hardly to need a commentary — driven by forces and appetites beyond their control, doomed in most cases to a tragic or inglorious fate, and with only fleeting gleams of the angel or the immortal in them. In his fictional world, therefore, impulses and desires are always "irresistible", attractions are "magnetic" and/or "fatal", antipathies are "instinctive", the male is a "slave" of the female (and vice versa) and is "inexorably" drawn to her (or to a male substitute), the greatest pleasure of the human being is to *see*, to be a *spectator* of others' misfortune (as though the strongest human emotion were curiosity), and human behaviour is limited, in its freedom, to a kind of animal choice among inevitable, generally unpleasant or degrading alternatives. Despite this tiresome reiteration of adjectives and concepts, there is little the translator can do to vary or palliate such a vocabulary. It bespeaks a world-view which is one of the factors that make the works of the great Naturalist authors (and Caminha, on the basis of two of his published novels, deserves to rank not unfavourably among them) so disturbing and so depressing, even now, a century after their writings began to appear.

I might quote here the warning of the Brazilian critic Valdemar Cavalcanti: "Accordingly, I advise no one to read this novel. I find it too corrosive, not so much because of its theme and contents but above all, because of the degree of pessimism it contains. It is a sombre book, with sombre characters, a sombre life!" But Caminha's pessimism, it should be remembered, is no blacker than that of Hardy, Zola, Eça de Queirós, or the master of the Brazilians, Machado de Assis, who wrote, at the end of *Memórias Póstumas de Brás Cubas* (*Epitaph of a Small Winner*) that he had done one good thing in life, had one credit to his account, that he had not "transmitted the misery of this existence to any other human being"; and, at the end of *Dom Casmurro*, that fate had so willed that "my dearest friend and the woman I loved best in life — both so loving, both so beloved — should join together to betray me" — a sort of heterosexual mirror image of the theme of *Bom-Crioulo*.

Bom-Crioulo was — and remains — a truly revolutionary work: revolutionary in its denunciation of slavery, sadism, cruelty and man's exploitation of man; revolutionary in its revelation of society's complicity, its conspiracy of silence, regarding all these abuses; revolutionary in its startling attitudes toward homosexuality, toward race, toward interracial and inter-age contacts. In the eighty-six years that have intervened since its publication (in a country whose traditional liberalism permitted such things to be published, even in those puritanical times — let due credit be given to the not-often-recognised "permissiveness" of that inchoate but great country, Brazil), it has lost little of its impact. Like Mary Shelley's *Frankenstein* and Goethe's *Die Wahlverwandtschaften* (*Elective Affinities*), it is one of the supremely idiosyncratic works of nineteenth-century fiction. Nevertheless, it belongs firmly to its times, and to their literary current — Naturalism. The world of the Naturalists *is* a sombre one, a world of closed doors and no exits, a world that allows no second chances, the natural predecessor of our doomed modern world. For this reason, if for no other, the story of the black slave who dared to dream of love, freedom and a world beyond race, sex and age, and learned too late that society would grant him none of these, only betrayal, imprisonment and discrimination, should be read and remembered. I could say, with Ford Madox Ford, "this is the saddest story I have ever heard." Its message echoes beyond our time.

BOM-CRIOULO

The Black Man and the Cabin Boy

I

The glorious old corvette, alas, was not even a memory of what she once had been, romantic and picturesque, the very ideal of sprightliness, like those legendary galley-ships of old, light and white on the high seas, calmly climbing the leaping, bucking waves!

She was different, very different now, with her blackened hull and mould-speckled sails. Nothing remained of the splendid warlike appearance that had swelled people's hearts with pride in the good old days when ships were ships and seamen were seamen. Seeing her from afar, in that endless stretch of blue, you would have said she was only the fantastic shadow of a warship. She had lost it all, that old floating hulk, from the clean, triumphant whiteness of her sails to the fresh paint that had once adorned her.

But still she went on, the ominous little boat, sailing the country's seas, almost mournful in her slow advance; still she went on, now no longer like a great white heron arrowing through that prairie of water, but slowly, heavily, like some large, apocalyptic bat with wings opened over the ocean.

She had just entered an area of doldrums. The sails began to flap slackly, weakly, swelling up with each swing, only to fall back, with a measured, muffled stroke, into their original somnolent langour. The trip was growing monotonous. The wide surface of the ocean spread out, shining and motionless under the rays of the midday sun, and the corvette barely inched along, so slowly, so imperceptibly that her movement could hardly be noticed.

No sign of any other ship on the blue line of the horizon, no mark of any human presence beyond that narrow ship-board. Water, only water all around, as if the world had disappeared in some catastrophic deluge. And high above, in the sky, the infinite silence of the spheres, blotted out by the day's rain of gold.

A melancholy, nostalgic seascape, where colours paled in the fierceness of the light, where the human voice was lost in a desolate immensity!

Sailors were talking in the prow of the boat, some of them sitting on the fo'c's'le, others standing, holding on to ropes or spreading their clothes out to dry in the sun, peacefully, resting from their labours. The metal plates of the masts, the cannon-breeches, the hatchway shafts, everything steel or bronze glittered blindingly, dazzling the eyes.

From time to time there was a great commotion. The rigging would begin to creak and groan, as though it were going to be torn away, the sails would beat tumultuously against the yards, ship's lines would hit against each other with dry little clicks, and the sound of water cascading against the belly of the old ship could be heard.

"Hold on, helmsman!" says a voice.

And the calm returns, and the apathy, the boredom, the endless doldrums go on.

The first symptoms of indolence could already be detected in the sailors' appearance: yawns and sleepy stretching of limbs, as before an afternoon nap. And the mountains of the coast and the consolations of home and family were still so far away!.

Food supplies were getting low and the days of jerked beef and canned food loomed threateningly: the sailors were becoming apprehensive.

The prow bell had just rung eleven.

The lieutenant on duty on the bridge checked with his pocket-watch, a fine gold precision piece which he had bought in Toulon, screwed up his moustache, looked at the watch again and, moving toward a sword that lay next to the mast, called, in a clear and slightly metallic voice:

"Bugler!"

He was a fine example of a naval officer — young, dark-skinned, with bright, intelligent eyes, a superb mathematician, a player of *Sueca*[1], and the author of an *Elementary Treatise on Practical Navigation*.

Nobody on board was better than he was at working out logarithms. He could calculate them with his eyes closed, and sines and co-sines flowed from the tip of his pencil in admirable fashion. He was always the first to determine the time of day, according to the ship's longitude. As soon as he'd graduated from the academy, he'd developed a reputation for his deep love both of mathematics and of naval life. As a midshipman he was

---

[1] *Sueca* or *sueca-duê* is a still popular game of trumps, a four-hand game played two against two in which a 40-card pack is used. The highest cards are the seven and the ace of each suit.

known to stay on board during shore-leave, "so as not to get out of practice". He was not fond of life on land and preferred to laze around in his cabin, among his books and photographs of ships and the sea, rather than waste his time in the exciting but unproductive activity of cafés and theatres.

"Bugler!" he repeated, frowning, with a sombre, severe expression on his face.

The order was repeated down the line by other voices, until finally there came running an exotic figure — a black sailor with very white eyes, exaggeratedly thick lips that opened in a vague, imbecilic smile, and a face whose features betokened both stupidity and subservience.

"At your orders, sir!" he said, raising his hand to his cap with a martial flourish.

"Call the men to muster," ordered the lieutenant.

At the first notes, clear and unechoing in the silence of the high seas, immediately there was a strange stirring in every corner of the ship. The sailors resting in the prow looked over their shoulders distrustfully at one another now. On the quarterdeck, on the lower decks, the movement increased as the bugle-call ended, with the voices of the guards rising above the din: "Up on deck, up on deck, everybody up on deck!" the whole mingling with the sound of clanking chains coming from the hold.

The bo's'n, a fussy dark-skinned mulatto, very proud of himself and of his glittering stripes and decorations, was lining the sailors up according to height, with the exacting exaggeratedness of a schoolteacher, pulling some out to replace them with others, warning this one because his shirt was unbuttoned, and that one because he didn't have a ribbon on his cap, and threatening another with bringing him up before the lieutenant because he wouldn't stand in line properly.

Officers began to appear in dress uniform — cap and epaulettes — trailing their swords, looking themselves over from head to toe, squeezed tight into their blue cloth sword-belts, worn over their uniforms.

Soon everyone was ready, sailors and officers — the former lined up in double rows on both sides of the ship, the latter astern, near the mainmast, with the respectful attitude of people who are going to attend a solemn ceremony.

Silence had fallen. A low voice here and there whispered timidly. And now, in the silence of the muster, the sound of water stubbornly dashing against the belly of the ship could be clearly heard.

27

"Hold on, helmsman!"

Finally the captain appeared, buttoning on his white chamois gloves, stiff in his new uniform, with an authoritative air, his sword dangling loose in elegant abandon, his epaulettes tossing on his shoulders in gold bunches, his whole person commanding respect.

He was a well-built man, of dignified features and appearance, severe-looking, very dark-skinned, with that burnt-in swarthiness, that bronze coloration, which the sun imparts to men of the sea, with a broad, bushy moustache, slightly graying, and with a touch of conventional arrogance in his attitude.

The silence among the ranks of sailors was total. A special gleam of indiscreet curiosity could be discerned in every eye. A tremor of instinctive cowardice, like an electric current, crossed the features of all those men crowded together there before a single man, whose words always bore the harsh stamp of discipline. It was a deep respect they felt, bordering on the subservience of an animal that squats and cowers to receive its punishment, just or unjust, whatever it may be.

"Bring in the prisoners," said the captain, impassively, pulling at the sleeve of his uniform.

All eyes turned, full of curiosity, toward the assistant artillery officer, as he hurried down the staircase to the lower deck, taciturn and unspeaking.

The lieutenant continued walking back and forth on the bridge, as if everything were running smoothly in that small floating world of which he, now, was a sort of temporary king. His slow, measured steps could be heard, like those of a sentry at night.

The blazing light of the sun fell from overhead, lending mica gleams to the great crystal of the still sea. A fierce, suffocating heat burned into the flesh, speeded up the circulation, congested and irritated the nervous system terribly, implacably.

The whole atmosphere seemed to pulse in a universal conflagration.

And the sail, wide and slack, flapped, flapped, like some desperate creature.

Damned doldrums! thought the lieutenant, scanning the horizon on all sides. For him, the exemplary sailor, to be caught like this, weather-watching, doing nothing, all because of this infernal, unending calm! That had very seldom happened to him. It was really enough to drive a man crazy.

The prisoners came in: a scrawny, smooth-faced, yellowish-skinned lad, without a trace of beard yet; another boy of about the same age, but a little darker, and a second-class sailor, a tall, broad-shouldered, sleek-faced black man.

They came in chained one to another, dragging their feet in short but long-drawn-out steps, and headed for the middle of the deck, stopping short at a signal from the captain. He immediately whispered something to another officer, who was at his side with a book in his hand, and, addressing the first culprit, the one who led the group, the yellowish, clay-faced boy, he asked:

"Do you know why you are going to be punished?"

The cabin-boy, without raising his head, murmured affirmatively: "yes, sir."

His name was Herculano, and in his beardless adolescent face there were hints of a quiet melancholy, as well as of a precocious and symptomatic morbidity, a secret sorrow.

On the square collar of his blue-flannel sailor shirt the white emblem of the cabin-boys stood out.

His fingernails were disgusting — tar-blackened and really uncared-for. His wretched appearance left a lasting and disagreeable impression.

The captain, after a short speech, in which the words "discipline and order" were repeated various times, gave a slight nod, and the first mate, moustached and blond, began to read the section of the Naval Code dealing with corporal punishment.

The sailors, rough and illiterate, listened in silence, with vaguely respectful expressions, standing in the hard, corrosive noonday light, to that oft-repeated chapter of the book of rules, while the officer on watch, who enjoyed the refreshing shade of a wide sun-blind strung over his head, came and went, from one side of the ship to the other, without worrying about the rest of humanity.

Next to the prisoners stood a very tall man, broad and muscular, the typical Amazonian half-breed,[1] in fatigues and cap and holding with both hands, against his resting knee, the instrument of punishment. He was Agostinho the guard, the famous Agostinho, a consummate expert in the art of caning, the strongest and bravest of all the guards. His pride in being a good sailor was legendary. When some difficult manouevre was being carried out, he was the one who helped the bo's'n at his job, always carrying a silver whistle, never shirking his obligations.

---

[1] *Caboclo*, a half-breed of mixed white-Indian, or sometimes white-Indian-Negro stock, native to the north of Brazil.

"That half-breed's a real man!" his fellow-sailors said.

If a block or any of the ship's lines came loose up in the rigging, in some dangerous spot, quick as a wink he'd bound up the ratlines, with that heavy body of his, he'd leap over the crow's nest, without looking back, and there he'd be, hanging from the beams, tying and untying ropes, light as a feather, the target of everyone's gaze, swaying with the ship, in danger of falling straight out into the sea. He was a close-mouthed man, who kept very much to himself, both tolerant and severe at the same time as far as his job of keeping order on ship went. He couldn't image running a ship without canings — "the only way to make a good sailor".

And he always had his maxim on the tip of his tongue: A warship without caning is worse than a merchant schooner.

For this very reason, the other sailors didn't like him; in fact, they avoided his presence and tried to stir up trouble between him and the bo's'n and the other officers of lower rank, with their commentaries: "Agostinho the guard's a really good man; he could take over a whole watch."

And among themselves they'd laugh in secret and curse "that ass Agostinho, who isn't even fit to be captain of a poop deck."

He was there too now, at his post, waiting for a signal to discharge his pitiless cane on the victim's body. He derived a special thrill from doing that. What the hell! Everybody has his own peculiarities.

"Twenty-five strokes," ordered the captain.

"With shirt off?" asked Agostinho right away, beaming, immensely pleased, bending his cane to test its flexibility.

"No, no; with shirt on."

And Herculano, free now from his shackles, sad and resigned to his fate, felt all the brute strength of the first blow on his back, while a voice chanted in a sleepy drawl:

"One!...and then, successively: "two!...three!... twenty-five!"

By then Herculano couldn't stand it any longer. He was standing on tiptoe, writhing, raising his arms and twisting his legs, wracked with pain that spread through his whole body, even to his face, pain so sharp that it felt as if his flesh were being torn from him. At every blow he uttered a muffled, trembling groan which he alone heard in the depths of his suffering.

The audience watched this scene without feeling the slightest pity, with the cold indifference of mummies.

"Rabble!" howled the captain, shaking his glove at them. "You don't take your duties seriously! You don't respect authority! I'll teach you! You'll learn or I'll cut you to pieces!"

It was a simple affair. Herculano had a strange way about him. He was always by himself, hanging around in corners, avoiding the other sailors' company, doing his job without talking to anyone, never joining in the *sambas*[1] at night in the prow. Timid and solitary, looking paler every day, with a dead gaze and noticeable dark shadows always under his eyes, with a tired voice, so weak that he could hardly stand up, he had earned the ridiculous nickname of "Drip".[2]

The poor cabin-boy could not stand for such a title, however harmless it might be, and he paid his fellow-sailors back by showering them with fishwifely obscenities which he had learned right there on board.

"Hey, Drip!"

That was enough to set him off and unleash his lexicon of insults, delivered in a threatening crescendo of fury that at times reached proportions of hysteria.

The other sailors, however, would simply split their sides laughing:

"There goes the Drip! Catch him!"

And the reply would be some obscenity, some rough insult, usually with reference to maternal ancestry.

One word leads to another, and almost always the joke would end in a totally different kind of situation, and the consequence would be detentions and punishments.

It so happened that, the evening before, Herculano had been caught by another sailor practising an ugly and depressing but very human act. He'd been found, all by himself, standing by the main rail, moving his arm to and fro in an awkward position, committing the most shameful of offences against himself.

The other sailor, a sly young mulatto, who used to go around at night spying on his fellow-sailors, to see what they were doing, hurried and called his friend Sant'Ana, and, lighting a match, they both came up to "have a look". The spot of still fresh sperm gleamed on the dock in the light. Herculano had

---

[1] The most popular form of musical expression in Brazil. The reference here would be to sessions of samba composing, playing (on the native musical instruments), singing and dancing, held in the prow at night during leisure hours.

[2] In the original, *Pinga*, which means "drop" or "white rum" or "penniless person".

31

just committed a real crime, one not listed in the rule-books, a crime against nature, pouring out uselessly, on the dry and sterile deck, the generative juice of man.

He was greatly embarrassed by being caught in the act, in such a grotesque situation. Wild with rage and white as a sheet, he attacked Sant'Ana, and in a little while the two were locked in combat, tumbling and kicking, awakening the other sailors who lay there sleeping the sweet sleep of the wee small hours. The affray ended with their both being locked up down in the hold.

"Ah! Mr. Drip, Mr. Drip!" repeated the guard on watch. "Don't think that you can get away with things just because you're white."

That was the crime committed by Herculano and his colleague Sant'Ana, who was also about to be punished.

Sant'Ana, however, wasn't the kind of boy to suffer in silence. He always had something to say when he was going to be punished, making whatever sly excuses he could to the authorities in order to escape justice: this never happened, for he was only too well known.

He was a poor devil of a third-class sailor, dark, walnut-skinned, with short, crewcut hair, black eyes, a flattened nose, and a gaunt face. His name had already been down in the punishment book a countless number of times. Afflicted with a congenital stammer, he could make his fellow-sailors laugh merely by opening his mouth to say something, especially when he was in one of his angry and over-excited moods, because, at such moments, nobody could understand him.

He was born also with a gift for turning on the tears. The slightest problem would make him weep, turning his eyes into two fountains of humid tenderness.

He immediately began now to stammer out a story of "provocations", of how he had been resting quietly in his corner when Herculano came and bothered him, "provoked him".

"Come on, guard, come on, it's getting late," said the captain. "I'm not here to listen to stories. Go ahead!"

Agostinho flexed his cane and resolutely, without asking any questions, with a little smile of instinctive viciousness visible at the corners of his mouth, unleashed the first blow.

"One!" counted the same voice as before.

The boy reared up on tiptoe, opening his eyes very wide and rubbing his hands together.

"Oh!" he groaned, with a cry of pain. "For...for...for the love of...of...of God, cap...cap...captain, sir!"

"Come on, come on!"

And the other blows followed, implacable, brutal as burning acids, falling one by one, painfully, on the cabin-boy's frail body.

All he could do was try to bear them all, one after another, because his cries, his pleas, his tears availed him nothing.

"I'll discipline you," roared the captain, in a sudden flash of fury and ill-humour, under the blazing light of the tropical noon. "I'll discipline you, you rabble!"

Not a tremor of agitation could be observed among the sailors, who had witnessed such scenes so often already that they no longer succeeded in producing any emotional effect in them, as though they were mere banal reproductions of some well-known picture.

A light and gentle breeze began to blow, so light that it barely alleviated the sun's burning strength. It swelled the sails almost imperceptibly.

The lieutenant, cheered a little by this breeze, which usually precedes stronger winds, was taking notes in a small notebook. He was eager to call the sailors back to work.

Almost noon, and the punishments weren't over yet.

The third prisoner followed, a tall, robust giant of a black man, a colossal, savage figure, defying, with his formidable set of muscles, the diseased softness and weakness of a whole decadent, enervated generation. His presence there, on this occasion, stirred great interest and lively curiosity: he was Amaro, the prow topwatch, known as Bom-Crioulo in shipboard slang.

"Come up closer", ordered the captain imperiously, hardening his voice and his features.

There was a distant humming, a light, timid murmuring in the ranks of the sailors, like the vague, uneasy sensation which takes hold of spectators at a theatre when the sets are being changed. Now things were really different. Herculano and Sant'Ana were only pipsqueaks, poor wretches of sailors who could barely take twenty-five strokes of the cane; they were just big children! What everyone was waiting to see was Amaro, the famous and terrible Bom-Crioulo.

Once again the Naval Code was read in the slow cadences of a religious rite, and the captain, drawing himself up in his splendid, perfectly-fitting uniform, asked:

"Do you know why you are going to be punished?"

"Yessir."

Bom-Crioulo pronounced these words in a resolute tone of voice, without a trace of uneasiness, his gaze boldly fixed on the gold stripes of the captain's uniform. He stood at attention, at the foot of the mast, heels together, arms rigid at his side. But in the line of his shoulders, in the way he held his head, in every part of his body there lurked the latent, menacing presence of an almost feline suppleness and dexterity.

For Bom-Crioulo was not just a strong man, not just one of those lucky organisms that possess the resistant qualities of bronze and that pulverise all opposition with the weight of their muscles.

Nervous strength was his intrinsic characteristic and asset, surpassing all his other bodily attributes, and it gave him an extraordinary, really invincible mobility, a rare, unpredictable, acrobatic quality.

He had further developed this precious gift of nature by making continuous use of it, a use that had made him well-known ashore, in fights with soldiers and boatmen, and on board, whenever he came back drunk from shore leave.

Because Bom-Crioulo drank his shot of rum[1] from time to time, and he even lowered himself so far as to go on binges that drove him to all kinds of crazy excesses.

He would arm himself with a knife and go to the docks, a completely changed man, his eyes darting fire, his cap pulled down on one side of his head, his shirt unbuttoned with the negligence of a madman, and then it was risky, it was downright rash for anyone to approach him. The black man was like a beast let out of a cage. Everybody ran away at his approach, sailors and boatmen alike, because nobody was in the mood to be beaten up.

Whenever there was a fight on the Pharoux dock,[2] everybody knew it was Bom-Crioulo versus the police. It attracted people; everybody in the neighbourhood came running, till the square was packed, as if some terrible tragedy had occurred. People took sides, for the police or for the navy. It was an indescribable confusion!

---

[1] In the original, *aguardente*, a synonym of *cachaça* or *pinga*. This alcoholic drink, distilled from sugar cane, and popular in all parts of Brazil, is sometimes referred to in English as "sugar-cane brandy."

[2] The Pharoux dock (*cais Pharoux*) is located in Rio de Janeiro at the foot of Palace Square (*largo do Paço*), between the Customs-House docks (*docas de Alfândega*) and the station for the ferry-boats (*Estação das barcas*) going to and from Niterói and the islands. This dock is where Bom-Crioulo habitually would land when coming to the city from the corvette.

The reason for his present imprisonment, however, on the high seas, on board the corvette, was different, completely different. Bom-Crioulo had barbarously beaten up one of the second-class sailors because the fellow had dared, "without his permission", to mistreat Aleixo the cabin-boy, a handsome little blue-eyed sailor-boy, who was everybody's favourite and about whom certain "things" were rumoured.

Shackled and chained in the hold, Bom-Crioulo didn't utter a word of protest. He was admirably meek when he was in his normal state of mind and not under the influence of alcohol, and he bowed to the will of authority and resignedly awaited his punishment. He realised that he had done wrong and that he should be punished, that he was no better than any other sailor, but — what the hell! — he was satisfied. He'd shown them once again that he was a man. And besides that, he was very fond of the cabin-boy, and he was sure that now he could win him over completely, the way one conquers a beautiful woman, a virgin wilderness, a land of gold. He was damn well satisfied!

The cane didn't leave a mark on him; he had a back of iron, strong enough to resist the powerful arm of Agostinho the guard as if he were a Hercules. He couldn't even remember any more how often he'd been caned.

"One!" chanted the same voice as before. "Two!... Three...."

Bom-Crioulo had taken off his cotton shirt, and, naked from the waist up, in a splendid display of muscles, his pectorals rippling, his black shoulderblades shining, a deep, smooth furrow running from top to bottom down the middle of his back, he didn't even utter a groan, as if he were receiving the lightest of punishments.

But he'd already taken fifty strokes of the cane! No one had heard a moan coming from his lips, no one had noticed any contortion, any gesture at all indicating pain. All that could be seen on that ebony back was the marks left by the cane, one on top of the other, crisscrossing like a great cobweb, purple and throbbing, cutting the skin in all directions.

But suddenly Bom-Crioulo shuddered and raised one arm. The cane had struck him full on the kidneys, affecting the lower stomach. It was a terrible blow, delivered with extraordinary force.

Agostinho trembled too, but he trembled with pleasure to see the triumph of his manual strength at last.

Sailors and officers alike, in an intent silence, followed every blow with the deepest interest.

"One hundred and fifty!"

Only then some of them noticed a red spot, a ruby drop, trickle down the sailor's black backbone, a drop which quickly turned into a ribbon of blood.

At that moment the officer on watch, focussing his spyglass, was trying to identify an almost invisible shadow which seemed to float at a great distance, on the farthest horizon: it might have been the smoke from some transatlantic liner.

"That's enough!" ordered the captain.

The punishment was over. Ship's work was due to start again.

II

It was still long, long before the abolition of slavery[1] when Bom-Crioulo, then known simply as Amaro, appeared, coming from God knows where, dressed in rough cotton clothes, his pack on his shoulder and a big straw hat on his head, wearing raw-leather sandals. Still a teenager (he must have been about eighteen) and knowing nothing of the difficulties facing any coloured man in a slave-based, profoundly superficial society like the Brazilian Empire,[2] innocent and determined, he had run away without even thinking of the consequences of his flight.

In those days the "runaway Negro" terrified the whole population to an unbelievable extent. People chased the errant slave like a wild animal, with spur and crossbow, following him into the jungle, leaping over chasms, swimming across rivers, climbing mountains. As soon as the disappearance of a slave was communicated to the authorities — help! help! — troops of horsemen scoured the woods, and couriers raced through the backlands with wondrous clamour, measuring footprints, spurring on the hunting dogs, smashing down coffee plantations. Doors were locked and bolted in fear and trembling. The third page of the newspapers always featured the drawing of a young runaway slave, his pack on his shoulder, and underneath came the "advertisement", almost always in large print, minute and explicit, with all the details, giving the height, age, distinguishing marks, bad habits and other characteristics of the fugitive. Besides all this, the "owner" would promise a generous reward to anyone who captured the slave.

Amaro succeeded, however, in eluding the vigilance of all interested parties. After the bitter experience of spending a night, the darkest night of his life, in a sort of cage with iron

---

[1] Slavery was abolished in Brazil only in 1888.

[2] The Brazilian imperial monarchy lasted from 1821 to 1889, under two emperors, Pedro I (1821-1831), son of King João VI of Portugal (which had previously ruled the country as a colony), and Pedro II (1831-1889), his son. In 1889 the empire was abolished and replaced by a republic.

gratings,[1] the young black man, whose only fear was of being returned to the "plantation", to the bosom of slavery, trembled with emotion at the sight of a very wide, very calm river, where boats and ships were being rowed in all directions, while others gave off plumes of smoke, and, far above, on the edge of the water, a high, pointed mountain, taller than he'd ever seen before, pierced the clouds.[2]

Then they made him take off all his clothes (he was really embarrassed), they checked his back, his chest, his genitals, and they gave him a blue sailor-shirt.

The same day he was sent to the Fort.[3] And as soon as the sloop, after a strong shove, pulled away from the dock, the new seaman felt his whole soul vibrate, for the first time, in an extraordinary fashion, as if the delicious coolness of some mysterious fluid had been injected into his hot African blood. Freedom poured in on him, through his eyes, his ears, his nostrils, through every pore, in short, like the very essence of light, sound, smell and of everything intangible. Everything around him: the blue plain of water singing against the sloop's prow, the pure blue of the sky, the distant profile of the mountains, the ships rocking among the islands, the motionless houses of the receding city — even his fellow-seamen, rowing with him in measured compass, as if they were all one single arm — and, above all, dear God, above all the wide, luminous expanse of the bay, in one word, the whole landscape, gave him such a strong sense of liberty and life that he really felt like crying, crying openly, frankly, before all the other men, as though he were going crazy. That magnificent sight, that landscape had burned itself into his mind forever; he would never again forget it, never again! The slave, the "runaway Negro" felt he was a real man, equal to other men, happy to be a man, as big as the world itself, with all the virile strength of his youth. And he felt sorry, he felt very sorry for those who'd stayed behind on the "plantation", working, working, without any salary, from crack of dawn till. . . God knows when!

---

[1] The young runaway slave has evidently been caught by a press-gang "recruiting volunteers" for the Brazilian navy.

[2] The "river" is actually Guanabara Bay, on which the cities of Rio de Janeiro and Niterói are situated, and which the first Portuguese explorers took for a river-mouth — hence Rio's name. The mountain is Sugar Loaf (Pão de Açúcar).

[3] Villegaignon Fort, the Brazilian Naval College, situated on Sergipe or Villegaignon Island, in Guanabara Bay. The island has now been joined to the mainland by landfill.

At the beginning, before he boarded his first ship, it had been hard for him to forget the past, to forget "mamma Sabina"[1] and the way of life he'd learned in the coffee groves. Many a time he even felt a vague longing to see and talk to his old fellow-workers. But soon these memories scattered, like the thin and distant smoke of burning cane-fields,[2] and he came back to reality, opening his eyes, with infinite pleasure, on the boat-encumbered sea.

Military discipline, with all its excesses, couldn't even be compared to the hard labour of the plantation, to the terrible rule of stock and whip. There was a world of difference. Here at least he had his hammock, his pillow and his clean clothes. And he ate well, he stuffed himself, like any citizen. Today there'd be a good side of boiled beef, tomorrow a delicious bean stew, Fridays, boiled codfish with hot sauce and red wine. Who could want more? And he was free, my God, free! Freedom alone was worth all the rest! Here they didn't care about a sailor's colour or his race. They were all equal, they all had the same privileges, the same duties, the same leisure time. And when your superior officers get to like you and you don't have any enemies, why, it's like living in heaven: nobody even thinks about tomorrow!

Amaro quickly found his way into his officers' affection. At first they could hardly keep from laughing at this strange recruit, who knew nothing of military discipline or customs, as wild as any savage. Everything he did, with his ingenuous green-horn ways, was simply hilarious. But after a few months they all realised "that nigger's going to be a good sailor." Amaro could handle a musket according to all the rules of the game. And he wasn't any dunce in artillery practice, either; he'd got a reputation as a "sharp-shooter".

Never, in this first year of apprenticeship, was it necessary to punish him for anything. His temperament was so gentle that the officers themselves began calling him "The Good Nigger", Bom-Crioulo. But his most fervent wish, his heart's desire, was to get on a ship, any ship, to become accustomed to living at sea, to get to know the ways of life aboard ship, while he was still young, to learn by practice how "to trim a yard, to reef a sail, to

---

[1] This is probably the Negro slave woman who suckled and cared for Amaro in childhood, quite likely not his own mother, since slave children were generally separated from their natural mothers at birth.
[2] In sugarcane-growing countries, it is customary to "refertilise" the field and drive away harmful animals (snakes, etc.), by burning it after harvesting the cane.

read the mariner's compass." He could very well be promoted right away. He envied sailors who travelled the high seas, far from land, veering and tacking freely through God's world. How good that air must be for the soul and body, that free air that you breathed out there at sea!

He amused himself by making little model ships of wood in the shape of battleships, with a pennant hanging from the topmast and portholes, miniature cruisers, tiny yachts, all of them carved out with his pocketknife and with the patience of an architect.

But they wouldn't give him a ship yet! Oh yes, he'd go on board sometimes, for practices, rowing across in the ship's boat, but he'd soon come back with the crowd of other apprentice sailors, sad because they hadn't let him stay, dreaming of stories of travel, things that he'd see, when he'd sail out for the first time beyond the harbour bar.

The day finally came. Bom-Crioulo was ordered to embark as a sailor on an old troopship that was going to the south of Brazil.

"Well, at last!" he shouted, raising his arms in a gesture of amazed and delighted surprise. At last, thank God, they remembered Bom-Crioulo!

And he went the rounds, happy as a lark, cheerful, all excited, telling everyone about his luck. Did anyone want anything from the south? Not even a souvenir of Rio Grande do Sul?[1] Nothing at all?

"Bring me back a girl from Paraguay, Bom-Crioulo," joked one.

"Look, I'd be happy with a dozen eggs from Santa Catarina."[2]

Others asked him for impossible things — a piece of fried "gringo,"[3] a bottle of Spanish blood, the ear of a "green-belly."[4]

---

[1] The southernmost state of Brazil, bordering on Uruguay/Argentina.

[2] A state of southern Brazil, immediately north of Rio Grande do Sul. Its inhabitants are of largely German ancestry and are known for their blue eyes and blond hair. This is the state Aleixo comes from.

[3] The word "gringo" in this context may mean any foreigner, for example, any one of the German, Spanish and Italian immigrants whose descendants largely people southern Brazil. However, it may also mean "Argentine" here; the people of Argentina commonly call all foreigners "gringos" and hence are referred to by their neighbours by the same name.

[4] The inhabitants of Santa Catarina state are popularly and jocosely referred to as *barrigas-verdes*, "green-bellies". The sobriquet comes from the green belt used by the legionnaires from the province in the War of the Cisplatine (1825-28).

And they all laughed at mess-hall, and they all hoped that Amaro would be happy and would enjoy his first trip and that he'd come back stout and strong, ready "to kill the Portuguese"[1] on the Mineiros dock.[2]

Some of them praised the captain of the troopship, old Novais, a good man, who disliked corporal punishment and was a real friend to the sailors.

And the first mate?

Well, the first mate was a chap called Pontes, who wore whiskers and who'd been in the wreck of the corvette *Isabel*; he was ugly as sin, poor fellow, but he was a good man; he wouldn't hurt a flea, either, just the opposite — a sailor who got in *his* good books was treated like a fine port wine.

Bom-Crioulo was delighted.

He was scheduled to go on board in the late afternoon, just before "striking the flag".

He was all ready, and you could see by his eyes, by his way of talking, by his gestures, how full of joy his heart was. It was a strange happiness, a feeling of well-being he'd never known before, almost like the first symptoms of a calm, harmless madness. It made him twenty times more a man than before; it made him feel stronger, more tested, ready for the trials of life. It was like a gentle drunkenness of the senses, the kind that stems from great joy or immense sadness. Bom-Crioulo had experienced such a feeling, such pleasure only once before, on the day when he had been forced to find out what freedom is, when he had been "recruited" by the navy. Now this freedom widened still further in his eyes, it grew disproportionately in his imagination, making him tremble, as though he were hallucinating, opening rose-coloured horizons, wide and unknown, in his soul.

---

[1]The Portuguese term used here is *galêgo*, which should refer to a native of Galicia, the far northwestern province of Spain. However, since Galicians speak a dialect, not of Spanish but of Portuguese, and physically resemble the Portuguese, and since both Galician and Portuguese immigrants abound in Brazil, they are considered by the more ignorant members of the Brazilian populace as one single race, referred to either as *galêgos* or as *portugas, portuguêses*, etc. A very strong popular prejudice exists in all Brazil, and particularly in the region of Rio de Janeiro, against both Portuguese and Galicians, who are the butt of much hostility and ill-will and many jokes, depreciatory appellatives, etc. This prejudice is quite evident in *Bom-Crioulo*.

[2]The Mineiros dock, on Guanabara Bay in Rio de Janeiro, is situated near the Benedictine monastery, São Bento, immediately to the north of the Customs-House docks .

He left behind him not a single enemy, not even a rival at the fort; he parted on good terms with everybody, self-absorbed in his own happiness, but full, too, of the irresistible nostalgia of someone who is going away.

When the sloop that was taking him moved away from the bridge, where his fellow-seamen were waving their caps at him, with touching enthusiasm, he felt a single tear trace its warm path down his cheek, and, to hide his emotion, he began to wave, too, standing up in the boat, watching the outline of the island[1] and the sailors saying goodbye to him disappear, little by little, in the mist of evening.

As he sat in the prow of the troopship, it seemed to him he could still hear, like the last memory of a dream, the voices of his comrades, hugging him and saying goodbye: "Goodbye, Bom-Crioulo, be happy!"

He couldn't sleep the whole night. Stretched out on his back on deck, as if he were in a soft, wide bed, he saw the stars disappear, one by one, in the half-shadow of the false dawn, and the day surge up again, gloriously, gilding the Organ Mountains,[2] painting the city buildings with gold, singing the triumphal hymn of resurrection.

And soon afterwards the magnificent backdrop of the bay had changed into a vast, shining desert of ocean, always unfolding in an endless circle of water, where not even the smallest oasis displayed its greenery. The grandeur of the sea filled him with a Spartan courage. There it was, all around him, the highest expression of infinite freedom and absolute dominion, concepts which he appreciated instinctively, vaguely, through a fog of ignorance.

Day followed day. Everybody on board liked him just as much as his friends at the fort, and the first time they saw him naked, one fine morning, after the decks had been washed down, relaxing with a salt-water bath, there was an uproar! That great body seemed absolutely boneless — the broad, hard chest, the arms, the stomach, the hips, the legs, all made up a formidable set of muscles, giving an impression of almost superhuman strength, which worked its fascination on the other sailors, who stared, smiling and open-mouthed, at the black man. From then

---

[1] Sergipe or Villegaignon Island, in Guanabara Bay, where the fort is located. Today it is linked to the mainland by the embankment where Santos Dumont airport was built.

[2] A mountain range located about 50 km. to the north of Rio de Janeiro, near the city of Teresópolis. The weirdly shaped and eroded rock cones of the range have given it its name.

on, Bom-Crioulo began to be considered a "man to be watched", exerting, as he did, a decisive influence on the spirit of the crew, who were simply obliged to recognise him as the strongest arm, the brawniest chest on board. He was the one called on to lift the heaviest weights. Bom-Crioulo was ready for anything, with his iron grip and the strength of his one-hundred-and-seventy-five pounds, ready to show how to hoist a main shroud, how to lower a sail in a storm, how to work with a will!

Meanwhile, his reputation was growing in the whole navy. "A real brute of a man, that Bom-Crioulo is", said the sailors admiringly. "A real animal, whole and hale, that's what he is!"

He still had one cherished desire. He longed to embark on a certain ship, whose captain, a member of the Brazilian nobility, was said to be particularly partial to well-built sailors; he was also known as an excellent trainer of young men and a perfect gentleman, severe but amiable in his dealings with his crew.

Bom-Crioulo knew him only by sight but had taken an immense liking to him. Besides, Captain Albuquerque rewarded good work; he was never unwilling to promote his favourites. The rumour that he preferred one sex to another in his amorous relations was probably just calumny and slander, like so many stories that people invent. As far as Bom-Crioulo was concerned, that was none of *his* business. That was a private matter. What the hell, *everybody* has some bad habit.

But the trip on the corvette was announced, and Bom-Crioulo left the troop-ship to pursue his new career.

He was about thirty years old by then, and he wore the insignia of a second-class sailor. If he personally had had the choice, he'd have preferred not to leave Rio de Janeiro any longer. In the intervening ten years he had travelled around almost the entire world, he had risked his life dozens of times, he had sacrificed himself without any result to show for it. And you finally get tired of it all. A poor sailor works like a dog, from morning to night, he spends sleepless nights, he puts up with insults and insolence from everybody, and he gets nothing out of it, nothing at all! The best thing to do was to take life as easy as possible.

Bom-Crioulo didn't have much better luck on this trip than he'd had on all his previous ones. He'd been named prow topwatch, a sort of supervisor of the foremast, and at first he discharged his duties faultlessly. Anyone could see the cleanliness and order he established there, from the masthead ring right down to the bronze of the belaying pins. The efficiency with which he performed his job was a sight to behold. The ship's work was always done in perfect order, without any hitches, as if the whole foremast were some great steam-driven machine, in a contest with the crews of the other masts.

But now, on the homeward trip, things had changed. The foremast was always one of the last to be ready, and there was always some problem, some difficulty. It would be a line that was stuck or a cable that was parting or something that was missing.

"Come on, get going!" the officer on watch would roar impatiently.

And only after a considerable lapse of time would Bom-Crioulo announce, from up on the topmast, in his hoarse voice: "Ready!"

Some said that rum was getting the better of the "nigger". But others hinted that Bom-Crioulo had become that way, forgetful and indifferent, ever since he "got mixed up" with Aleixo, the cabin-boy, the beautiful little blue-eyed sailor-boy, who'd signed on in the south of the country. That devil of a Negro was really getting brazen! And no giving him advice or scolding him. He was a real man and perfectly capable of wiping the deck with anyone!

Even the captain knew about his scandalous friendship with the lad. He feigned indifference, as though he weren't aware of anything, but you could see in his eyes a certain anticipatory gleam, as if he'd love to catch them in the act.

The officers gossiped about the affair in lowered voices and often laughed maliciously about it between sips of lemonade, in the gun-room.[1]

But no one had anything but suspicions to go on, and Bom-Crioulo, with his brutish appearance, with a permanently bloodshot left eye, with his wide face and jutting jaw, was not particularly concerned about other people's opinions. Just so long as nobody said anything about it to his face, because, if they did, then there'd be hell to pay. The cane was invented for the sailor, and he'd take it until it killed him, like a stubborn animal, but he'd show them what it was to be a man!

Besides, his friendship for the cabin-boy had begun unexpectedly, like all really profound affections, without any kind of prelude, at the fatal moment when each caught the other's gaze for the first time. That indefinable movement toward each

---

[1] The gun-room was the officers' mess and common-room. It was so called because, in older warships, the weapons used by sailors and officers were kept here, in cupboards.

other which invades and impels two beings of opposite sex at the same time and determines their bodily desire for possession of each other, that animal attraction that makes man woman's slave and that, in every species, drives the male toward the female — that was what Bom-Crioulo felt, irresistibly, when he first caught sight of the little cabin-boy. He had never felt anything like it before. No man or woman had ever produced such a strange effect on him in his whole life! In any event, all that can be said is that the boy, a mere child of fifteen, had shaken his very soul, dominating him, enslaving him on the spot, at that very instant, with the binding force of a magnet.

He called the boy over, his voice full of tenderness, and asked his name.

"My name's Aleixo, sir," said the cabin-boy, lowering his eyes, new on the job and unsure of himself.

"Poor little fellow, his name's Aleixo," repeated Bom-Crioulo.

And immediately, without taking his eyes off the boy, he said, in the same soft, affectionate voice:

"Well, listen. I'm called Bom-Crioulo, don't forget the name. If anybody bothers you or does anything to you, I'm here to defend you, understand?"

"Yessir," said the little sailor, raising his eyes with an expression of gratitude.

"You don't need to be bashful, not at all. I'm Bom-Crioulo, the prow topwatch. All you have to do is call on me."

"Yessir."

"One more thing," the black man went on, taking the boy's hand. "Be very careful with everything you do, so you won't get punished, all right?"

Aleixo only answered timidly, "Yessir" — with the innocent air of an obedient child, with his very clear, speckled, light-blue eyes, and thick, extremely red lips.

He was the son of a poor family of fisherfolk, who'd signed him on board in Santa Catarina, and he was just reaching adolescence. His duties on board consisted in collecting the ropes and scouring the bronze and other metal parts of the ship, and sometimes being on watch at night.

He was afraid of Bom-Crioulo at first; in fact, Bom-Crioulo had almost made him cry one time, when he caught him out, smoking alone with the assistant prow man on the lower deck. The look that black man had given him! Luckily nothing came of it. But from then on Aleixo, without realising it, gradually became accustomed to those little kindnesses, to that warm-hearted interest in him, which didn't blink at sacrifices or balk at spending money on him. And, with time, he developed a definite soft spot in his heart for Bom-Crioulo; he was visibly beginning to feel a sincere, grateful affection for the sailor.

That was when the black man, in his enthusiasm over his new friendship, chose to show the cabin-boy how important he was on board among the other men, and how far he was willing to go for him, in his eagerness and his impassioned egotism, by brutally beating up the second-class man who had treated Aleixo badly.

The idea that Bom-Crioulo had suffered physically for him made such an impression on the cabin-boy's mind and heart that he now considered him a true, unselfish protector, a friend of the weak and oppressed.

Coming back from that long trip south, Bom-Crioulo was stronger, more vigorous and more of a man than ever. He was a brute mass of muscles at the service of a magnificent human mechanism. With respect to discipline, he'd also changed somewhat. He no longer displayed the former scrupulous obedience and seriousness. He had lost even that modest, respectful attitude which had earned him the good opinion of the officers at the fort and which distinguished him from the mass of undignified, undisciplined sailors. He had definitely gone over to their side; he'd left, somewhere on the high seas or in the ports he'd visited, that docile, easy-going temperament he had possessed. Now he treated his superior officers with scorn, taking advantage of them if they gave in to his wishes, cursing them when they weren't around, saying they were unjust and spiteful. But he had kept one quality — his physical strength, by means of which he controlled the other sailors more and more: no one dared to take him on, even as a joke. His reputation for courage and manliness had spread so far and wide that even on land, in the provincial cities, people talked with a grain of caution about "Bom-Crioulo". Was there *anyone* who hadn't heard of him, good Lord? And incidentally, he'd been a slave, and the damned nigger wasn't even so bad looking when you came right down to it.

After the troopship in which he'd made his maiden voyage he was assigned to a cruiser that had just arrived from Europe. Things didn't go so smoothly for him there. Captain Varela, a man more severe and unbending than any other officer of his generation, who never laughed, called him to account one fine day, simply because Bom-Crioulo had hit another sailor over the head with an oar over some trifling matter relating to work, and almost left Bom-Crioulo speechless. That was his first punishment in four years of service. Profoundly offended, he made an effort now to appear lazy and rebellious; full of resentment, he no longer took his duties seriously, as he had done before, working "for the good name of the company" without getting annoyed or feeling he was being exploited. Anybody who killed himself working was crazy. Sailors that did no work drew their salary just like the ones that worked. Sons of bitches!

So he gradually became contrary and difficult, concerned more with his own interests than with anything else, spending one month in hospital on sick leave and the next on board, or in the city, on shore leave.

III

A fresh, revivifying wind, fortunately, succeeded the equatorial-like calm of the previous day, wrinkling the wide surface of the water, swelling the sails and giving every face a new look of good humour and cheerfulness.

The sky was a brilliant, cloudless blue, immense and high in the eternal glory of light. Little white-necked birds followed along with the corvette, lighting on the water, ceaselessly-moving harbingers of good fortune, their noisy glee mingling with the muffled swelling of the waves, in a rapid flap of wings.

Now, at last, all the sailors were happy, in hopes of arriving soon, safe and sound, in Guanabara Bay, where there was peace and plenty, where life was sweet and full of ease and tranquillity, because they were near their families, just across the water from the city, without all the insecurity of a traveller on the open seas. And it was high time, after all! Twenty boring days veering and tacking to and fro, without even sighting land, not even an island, leading a dog's life! It was high time.

Only one person on board wished that the trip would go on forever, that the corvette would never arrive, that the sea would suddenly rise and submerge islands and continents in a tremendous inundation in which only the old ship, like some phantom, would survive, and she alone would go on floating, noble and indestructible, for all eternity. That person was Bom-Crioulo, the black man Amaro, whose spirit was struggling, like a bird in agony, with one single obsessive idea — Aleixo, the cabin-boy, who no longer let him think of anything else, who tortured him painfully. Unlucky hour when the boy set foot on board! Up until then his life had run its course as God had intended it to, more or less peacefully, without major inconveniences and troubles, sometimes happy, sometimes sad, it's true, but nothing is certain in life, and, at all events, he went on living. But now? Now...oh, oh!...now it couldn't be helped. What was going to happen had to happen.

And he thought of the boy, with his blue eyes, with his blond hair, his soft, plump curves, his whole tempting being.

In his leisure hours, when he was on the job, whether it rained or whether fire fell from heaven, nothing and no one could get the boy off his mind. It was a constant obsession, a fixed, stubborn idea, a weakness of his will, which was irresistibly dominated by the desire to unite himself to the sailor-boy as though he were of the opposite sex, to possess him, to have him by his side, to love him, to enjoy him!

At this thought, Bom-Crioulo would become incredibly transformed; he'd feel that burning desire sting his flesh like the prick of a needle, like spines of wild nettle — a Tantalus-like thirst for forbidden pleasures that seemed to sear his nerves and his whole body, outside and inside.

He couldn't remember ever having been in love before or even having ventured on one of those affairs with prostitutes that are so common in young men's lives. No, on the contrary; he had always been indifferent to things like that, and had preferred carousing with the boys right there on board, far from women's intrigues and deceits. He recalled only two exceptions to the almost virginal purity of his life and habits, and they had both happened by a sort of miraculous accident. When he was twenty, he was unexpectedly forced to sleep with a girl in Angra dos Reis,[1] near the waterfalls, and his performance as a man on that occasion had, incidentally, left a great deal to be desired. Some time after that, once, in a state of complete drunkenness, he had knocked on the door of a French prostitute's house in Rocio Square.[2] He had come out of that house quite ashamed of himself and had sworn never again to have anything to do with "those things".

And now, why was he lacking in strength to resist the impulses of his blood? How could anyone conceive of love, of the desire for animal possession, between two people of the same sex, between two men?

All this revolved confusedly in his mind, upsetting his ideas, contradicting the evidence of his senses, reawakening scruples. Of course he wouldn't be the first person on board to set the example, if the boy were willing to go along with him. But —

[1] A port near Rio de Janeiro, in a narrow strip of land between the sea and the Ariró range. The Portuguese of André Gonçalves arrived at the cove (angra) on the 6th January 1500, hence the name.
[2] Largo do Rocio, where now is Praça Tiradentes (Tiradentes Square), with its famous theatre (Teatro Real de São João) and many cafés, was at the time a centre of night-life.

whether by instinct or lack of experience — something in him was shocked by the idea of such an immoral act, which, nevertheless, various of his superior officers practised nearly every night right there on deck. Hadn't he been getting along very nicely without "that"? Well, then what the hell! It wasn't right to take advantage of the cabin-boy; he was just a child. Whenever he felt the need of "that", there were girls from every country in the world in Rio de Janeiro — Frenchwomen, English girls, Spanish girls. The choice was up to him!

He'd fall into introspection, remorseful and listless, gnawed by scruples about everything, trying to decide what was the correct course of action, filled at times with a languid and compassionate tenderness — his vagrant gaze lost in the seamless blue sky.

The punishment he had undergone for Aleixo's sake had had another negative consequence. The same day, he was replaced as prow topwatch; but that was really a relief, a rest from so much work. Whatever the officers decided was fine with him, just so long as they left him undisturbed in his nook and in his daily routine. He'd never asked favours of anyone.

"Listen", he would say to the cabin-boy, with a touch of irony in his counsellor's voice: "Don't get mixed up with the officers. They're all very nice, they're very friendly so long as they need you, just so long as they need you, but when they don't need you any longer — it's goodbye! — and they kick you in the teeth."

Aleixo was very happy with the life he was leading on the corvette, under the open blue sky; he was well-treated, he was well-liked, he was envied by not a few of his colleagues. He had everything he wanted, absolutely everything. He was a sort of little prince among the cabin-boys, the apple of the officers' eyes: they called him "boy", in English. He quickly became accustomed to the wandering life of a sailor and began to lose his bashfulness and his former timidity. Anyone who saw him now, nimble and lively, eager and enthusiastic at ship's work, always neat and clean in his white uniform, his cap to one side, his shirt unbuttoned a little in front, revealing the hollow of the neck below the larynx, couldn't help really liking him and wishing him well. This rapid metamorphosis, almost without a transition period, had been the work of Bom-Crioulo, whose advice almost effortlessly captured the cabin-boy's heart and mind, awakening in his innocent, childlike soul the desire to win sympathies, to attract the attention of others to himself.

Boasting of his knowledge of "the world", Bom-Crioulo first took pains to flatter Aleixo's vanity. He gave him a cheap little mirror that he'd bought in Rio de Janeiro — "so you can see how good-looking you are". The boy looked at himself in the mirror, smiled and lowered his eyes. Good-looking! He thought he looked like a ram with its horns cut off! But he kept the trinket; he stored it away carefully in the bottom of the hammock chest,[1] like someone guarding a rare and precious object, and every morning he would look at himself, sticking out his tongue, examining himself carefully, after having washed his face.

Bom-Crioulo saw the effect of his experiment and tried to complete the young sailor's "education". He showed him how to knot his tie properly (not a tie, he said, that's not called a tie, you call it a "kerchief"). He advised him never to wear his cap on the top of his head — a sailor should always wear his cap to one side, with a certain amount of stylishness.

And what about the shirt? Oh, well, the shirt should be unbuttoned a little at the neck, to show the one underneath, the knit shirt. Clothes make the man.

The cabin-boy took all this advice like a son, without even asking about the reason for so much care and attention. He saw dirty, badly-dressed, sweaty-smelling sailors, but there weren't too many of them. Some of them even used perfume on their kerchiefs and lotion on their hair.

In a few days, Aleixo was like a different person. Bom-Crioulo looked at him with the pride of a teacher watching a pupil's development.

One fine Sunday, when everybody had to turn out in a white uniform, according to the order of the day, the cabin-boy was the last person to come up on deck for muster. He was perfect, irreproachable, in his tropical uniform, his blue shirt-collar stiff with starch, wearing bell-bottom trousers, cap to one side of his head, his high-laced boots well-shined.

Bom-Crioulo, who was already up on the quarterdeck, was so dazzled when he saw the boy, dressed so elegantly, that he nearly did something really foolish. He felt like hugging the boy tight, right there before the whole crew, like devouring him with kisses, crushing him under his own body with the weight of his caresses. Yessirree! He looked just like a girl in that uniform. He was really p-e-r-f-e-c-t! So the mirror had really done its good work, eh?

---

[1]In older ships, the "hammock chests" were a series of chests or cupboards, built along the ship's wall, where the sailors' hammocks and other belongings were kept.

And with a quick, nervous gesture, trying to hide his lust, he murmured:

"You beautiful kid!"

The boy, far from being put out by the compliment, looked himself up and down, smilingly, smacked his lips in mock disdain and went off to take his place in the ranks without saying a word.

Later, after the Naval Regulations had been read, after the sailors had passed muster, Bom-Crioulo called the boy to the prow, and they engaged in a long conversation, which must have been a delightful experience for the black man, judging by the ever-widening, beaming smile on his face.

The sea was relatively calm, barely ruffled by a light breeze that alleviated the day's sultriness. Cumuli piled up in the south, growing into black nimbi, as though all impelled by one and the same force, but still far distant, level with the horizon. Above, in the dome of the great half-sphere of the sky, ablaze with noonday light, the blue, always the clear blue, the pure blue, the sweet, transparent, infinite, mysterious blue. The corvette must have been quite near land, because on the horizon there passed the triangular sail of a *jangada*,[1] tiny and rapid. Behind, on the starboard side, the dark bulk of a huge, double-chimneyed steamship was gaining on them also.

Bom-Crioulo and Aleixo went on with their conversation, sitting side by side in the shadow of the jib sail, indifferent to the laughter and merriment of the other sailors, whose attention was being drawn now to the steamship. All of them, except those two friends, were wondering what nationality the "brute" was. Some swore that she was English, because of her size; others thought that the two colours of her smokestacks indicated she belonged to *Messageries Maritimes*. She must be the *Equateur* or the *Gironde* — either one of the two. They laid bets, as the enormous ship approached, and the little *jangada* slowly disappeared from sight.

"But listen, don't you try to go running around with anybody else," Bom-Crioulo was saying. "Rio de Janeiro is a wicked, wicked city. If I catch you with somebody else, you know what's in store for you."

The young lad chewed absent-mindedly on the tip of his blue calico kerchief with white spots, listening to the older man's

---

[1] A type of wooden raft, fitted out with a sail and capable of surprisingly high speeds, much used by Brazilian fishermen, especially in the northeast of the country.

promises, dreaming of a rose-coloured future in that oh so famous city of Rio de Janeiro, where there was a huge mountain called Sugar Loaf[1] and where the emperor had his palace, a beautiful mansion with walls of gold.

Everything took on exaggerated proportions in the imagination of this sailor-boy on his first trip. Bom-Crioulo had promised to take him to the theatres, to Corcovado (that was another mountain, from which you could see the whole city and the sea), to Tijuca, to the park called Passeio Público, everywhere. They were going to live together, in a room on Misericórdia Street,[2] a room that would cost fifteen *mil-reis*[3] a month, where there'd be room for two iron beds, or maybe just one, if it were wide and spacious. Bom-Crioulo would pay for everything out of his own salary. They could live a peaceful life there. If they stayed together on the same ship, it would be the best possible arrangement. But if, by bad luck, they were separated, they'd find a way. Nothing in this world is impossible.

"And you don't need to go around telling anybody about this", the black man said, finally. "Mum's the word: just leave it to me and I'll handle everything."

At this precise moment the great steamship was face-to-face with the corvette, showing the colours of the British flag astern, like one of those big red kerchiefs for snuff users; and three fearful blasts on her whistle saluted the little warship, whose flag also fluttered astern, green and gold.

A crowd of people milled around in the prow of the English steamer, no doubt Italian immigrants on their way to Brazil. The captain could easily be seen, on the bridge, with his white uniform and his cork hat, spyglass in hand. Handkerchiefs waved at the corvette, which quickly fell behind, all sails billowing, slow and proud.

And the liner disappeared like a shadow, and the corvette continued on in her defeat, alone in the emptiness of the sea, mournful and desolate. The sailors had scattered about on the

---

[1] Pão de Açúcar, Sugar Loaf Mountain, is a large granite rock, some 375 metres high, now provided with a cable-car for ascent, situated at the entrance to Guanabara Bay.

[2] This street, which still exists in part, begins behind 15th of November Square (praça 15 de novembro) and takes its name from the old Mercy or Charity Hospital (Santa Casa de Misericórdia) on Mercy Square (largo da Misericórdia).

[3] A former Brazilian unit of currency [the Portuguese one had the same name], the *mil-réis*, divided into one thousand *réis*, was replaced in 1942 by the *cruzeiro*, divided into one hundred *centavos*.

various decks, busy at their work, waiting for the four o'clock meal bell.

The mountain of clouds that just a little earlier had reared up, phantasmagorically, far in the distance, to the south, was covering the sky now and coming ever nearer, leaden-coloured, stormy, unfolding into strange shapes and forms, like an enormous barrier that had suddenly appeared between the corvette and the horizon. Half-obscured already, the sun filtered its melancholy light through the clouds, crisscrossing them with a brilliant, multicoloured rainbow, like a saint's halo, that descended toward the sea.

The storm was imminent.

"Man the top-gallant sails and skysails!" shouted the officer on watch.

A general mobilisation followed his shout. Whistles shrilled immediately, and the quarterdeck was flooded with sailors and officers who came swarming tumultuously up the hatchways, running and pushing one another. The figure of Agostinho the guard was clearly visible in the prow, calm and grave, checking the rigging.

"Lower that sail, furl that sail!"

The whistles shrilled again, in the desperation of manoeuvres that had to be performed too quickly. Avalanches of sailors rushed from one side of the ship to the other, hauling in ropes, bumping into one another in their haste, like savage hordes, stampeding, all this to the accompaniment of the noise of blocks squeaking like country oxcarts.

"Hold on to the rudder, helmsman!" warned the officer on watch, muffled in his waterproof cape.

The sky had grown completely dark, and the gale picked up and began to whistle sinisterly through the rigging, with the extraordinary strength of an invisible giant. Sea and sky ran together in the darkness, forming a single element of blackness around the corvette, enclosing it in all directions, as if everything in it were fated to disappear under the weight of water and clouds...Great high-flying waves passed, roaring under the keel, dancing a frightening, dizzying dance around the prow every time the ship's belly plunged into the water, at the risk of splitting open down the middle. Sheets of rain inundated the deck, forcing the sailors to roll up their trouser-legs and drenching the piles of rope, in an unexpected general washing-down.

The corvette was left with only topsails and mizzen-sail operating. It scooted now along the surface of the sea as though it were a mere yacht, a pleasure-craft, light, its sails full-bellied in the wind, riding the waves, its sides almost level with the water.

What glory for the officer on watch! How good he must have felt at that moment, under his waterproof cape, drenched right to the toes, his whole being alert and attentive so that the ship would not go off course, full of a sense of responsibility, on the job, calmly doing his duty, while the other officers relaxed in the gun-room! Now and then he'd look back astern and would see, with the greatest of pleasure, the long wake of foam which the corvette was leaving behind it. He felt strong, he felt like a real man! Definitely, he thought, the navy is the best school for courage.

The squall lasted for an hour and a half, with a heavy, persistent rain, blowing the wrong way, which seemed as though it would never end. Suddenly the clouds opened on a clear blue sky. The light once again illuminated the horizons, and little by little the last remnants of the "bit of fun" disappeared — as Lieutenant Souza, the officer who had earlier been cursing the doldrums and who was due to go on watch now, later called it.

But the wind continued blowing hard, whipping the ship's lines, raking the surface of the water, moaning sad melodies like some fantastic cello, in gusts that shook the whole ship.

Ten knots the ship was doing, ten knots an hour.

"Watch that rudder, helmsman!"

Sailors swept down the deck, while others swabbed the parts where there was no longer any water. From up above, from the quarterdeck, the voices of the officers could be heard, chatting on the broadside, sitting there in picturesque disorder, smoking and laughing. The paymaster,[1] a thin fellow with long whiskers, was studying the clarinet, down below, in the gun-room, with admirable patience, trying to keep his balance. The rain had refreshed everybody, men and officers alike, reviving them all physically.

Bom-Crioulo, tired of working, had gone down to the lower deck and was talking too, to Aleixo, whom he'd left only when he had to go about his work.

The dampness, the chill that came in through the hatchways, that frigid atmosphere imbued him with an almost insane desire for physical love, an irresistible sense of softness and weakness.

---

[1] The paymaster, on older ships, was an official in charge of the ship's finances, somewhat similar to the present purser.

Joined to the cabin-boy in what was almost a hug, his hand on the shoulder of Aleixo, who had a vague sensation of being caressed by that contact, Bom-Crioulo forgot about all his fellow-seamen, forgot everything around him and thought only about the cabin-boy, his "beautiful little kid" and about the future of that inexplicable friendship.

"Were you very scared?"

"Of what?"

"Of the storm."

"No, not at all."

And Aleixo took advantage of the opportunity to tell a story about a "southeaster" in Santa Catarina. He and his father had gone out fishing in a dug-out canoe, around noon, one day. Suddenly, the sea began to foam and the wind started to blow, and what were they going to do? They were alone near Rat Island in a dug-out that was like a nut-shell. His old man, God bless him, didn't doubt for a minute: he grabbed the oars and — glub-glub, glub-glub, glub-glub. "Hold on, my son!" And the wind blowing stronger and stronger, whistling in your ears like the devil himself. Then came a sudden gust, a terrible blast of wind, and when Aleixo tried to grab hold of his father, it was too late: the dug-out turned over!

Bom-Crioulo pretended to be greatly astonished:

"It keeled over?"

"It certainly did keel over, and then what happened? I know I went right down to the bottom, and I came up again. Then I don't remember anything. When I woke up, I was on the beach, safe and sound, thank God!"

"You were really lucky," said the black man in an interested tone. "You might've drowned."

And Bom-Crioulo had his stories to tell, too, and the conversation went on till nightfall, when they all went up on the quarterdeck to divide up the ship's work for that night.

But instead of letting up, the "southeaster" was blowing harder than ever, strong and stubborn, threatening to tear off every piece of rope and every shred of canvas. The corvette, the "old skiff", as they called it, was speeding dizzily through those stormy seas, pitching and tossing gently, shaking at times, when the waves were at their highest, with its two coloured lanterns — the red one to starboard, the green one to larboard — and the little foresail lantern, pale and tiny, high up on the jib stay.

Still with only topsails and mizzen-sail raised, with the wind driving it from astern, the old ship, huge and dark in the bright night, ghostly and silent, sped desperately towards its native land.

The moon, rising slowly, slowly, a fiery red at first, then cold and opalescent, more a blend of mist and light, the very essence of solitude, cast a veil of melancholy over the long seascape composed only of waves, shedding on the water that caressing light, that ideal glow that penetrates the heart of the sailor and fills him with the infinite nostalgia of the man of the sea.

And that wind wouldn't die down!

At that rate, they'd be back on land soon enough. Maybe one more day.

Waiting for the dreary hour of curfew, of sleep, which continued till the break of dawn, the sailors gathered in the prow to pass the time away, singing backwoods melodies to the tune of a mournful guitar,[1] laughing, tap-dancing, competing to see who was the best at making up their poor, primitive, badly-rimed verses, their "country ballads". A full moon like this one couldn't be wasted! They had worked hard; they needed to relax, too. Stretched out on deck, some lying on their backs, others on their stomachs, with their hands under their heads — one seated quietly, another, with his legs crossed, smoking — all of them completely free, at liberty, they formed a sort of circle around the fo'c's'le, while it was still early.

The officer on watch, endlessly walking back and forth, listened to them and was touched by their music. He mused over the fate of those poor chaps without home or family, who died singing, far from all human affection, sometimes far from their country, wherever their fate led them. Those crude, improvised songs, almost without rime or metre, possessed, nevertheless, the sharp flavour of wild fruit, the mysterious charm of innocent confessions. It did the heart good to hear them; they made it swell and overflow with a surge of sad yet consoling nostalgia.

Let them sing, poor devils of sailors, let them forget all the uncertainties of the life they lead — let them sing!

The guitar laments, and a soul sobs in each bass-string; songs echo into space like a challenge in the infinite silence of the

---

[1] The instrument referred to, called in Portuguese *viola*, is a stringed instrument, played with the fingers, similar in form and sound quality to the guitar. It was introduced into Brazil by the Jesuits and is the invariable accompaniment, in all parts of the nation, of country music, popular dances, etc. The number of strings, the tuning, the wood used, etc., vary from one region of the country to another.

moonlit night.

Time flies, nobody notices what time it is, everyone forgets to go to sleep, no one closes his eyes on the cold translucent seascape of tropical moonlight swept by a south wind. It was a mysterious instrument, that guitar; it made men forget the pains and troubles of life; it enchanted the soul; it strengthened the spirit!

Bom-Crioulo didn't take part in the celebration. He was tired of hearing popular songs. The days had long passed when he liked to court the girls and dance the *baião*,[1] making all the other young blades roar with laughter as he did so.

And when the little prow-bell struck nine o'clock, they saw him steal cat-like away, with his hammock under his arm. He passed by quickly, avoiding the glances of the other sailors, silent, impenetrable, sombre. He ran down the stairs of the hatchway and disappeared on the lower deck.

What did he intend to do? Commit some crime? Some treacherous act? Nothing of the sort. Like any other human being, Bom-Crioulo tried to make himself as comfortable as possible. Hell, up on the quarterdeck the wind would turn a man to ice! The lower deck was always a bit warmer. God helps those that help themselves.

He unfolded his hammock, stretched it out cautiously on the deck, the way a woman would, checked the sheet and, taking off his blue flannel shirt, he lay down with a long sigh of contentment. Ah, this was the way he wanted to be now. To all a good night!

Not even a voice broke the compulsory silence of the curfew, except that of the officer on watch, every hour on the hour, calling:

"Night watch!"

The wind was still blowing hard.

Both upper and lower decks looked like a nomads' camping-ground. The sailors, benumbed by so much work, had all fallen into a deep slumber, stretched out here and there in the cold night dew, as disorderly as gypsies that don't even have a fixed place to sleep. Little did they care about the wet boards beneath them, about the chilly draughts, the colds they'd surely get, about beri-beri. The confusion was even greater on the lower

---

[1] *Baião* or *baiano* is a Brazilian dance and musical form used only in the North of the country from Bahia up to Maranhão. It is similar to *lundu* with two differences: it allows of improvisation and is purely instrumental (even if meant to be sung).

deck. Canvas hammocks, dirty as old dishrags, dangling from iron bars, one above another, swayed to and fro in the feeble, dying lantern-light. Try to picture the hold of a merchant ship, carrying a cargo of human misery. In the spaces between the guns, in the half-darkness of hollows, indistinct, semi-naked forms turned and stirred. There was a sickening prison smell that you breathed everywhere, the acrid odour of human sweat mingled with urine and tar. Black men, open-mouthed, snored heavily, their bodies twisting in the unconscious movements of sleep. Nude bodies could be seen, clutching the deck, in indecent postures which moonlight cruelly spotlighted. Now and then a sleeper's voice muttered unintelligible statements. A sailor got up from among his fellows, totally naked, his eyes bulging, terrifying in aspect, screaming that they were going to kill him. It turned out that the poor devil was merely having a nightmare. Silence returned.

And above, on the bridge, the officer on watch, vigilant and imperturbable, called from hour to hour:

"Night watch!"

Then there would be a slight stirring. The guard would blow his whistle to wake up those who were going on duty: "Up, up! You're on watch now!" — and the monotonous night hours would go on this way.

Bom-Crioulo had no duties that night. His mind had not been at peace all that afternoon, as he mulled over and over schemes for conquering the cabin-boy once and for all, for giving expression, at long last, to his uncontrollable male desire, tormented by Greek carnality.

At times he'd tried to sound out the cabin-boy, seeking to win him over, to get him physically excited. But the boy would act hard-to-get, gently rejecting, like a young girl in love, certain overtures the black man made. "Stop that, Bom-Crioulo, and act serious for a change!"

On that day, however, Priapus resolved to end the struggle. It was do or die! Either his young friend made up his mind, or everything was over between them. They had to settle "those things".

"What 'things'?" asked the boy, in wide-eyed surprise.

"Oh, nothing, but I don't want you to get angry with me."

And then, suddenly:

"Where're you going to sleep tonight?"

"Away up in the prow, on the lower deck, because it's so cold."

"Well, we'll talk about things later."

59

At nine o'clock, when Bom-Crioulo saw Aleixo going downstairs, he grabbed his hammock and quickly followed the boy. That was when the other sailors saw him go by with his things under his arm, stealing cat-like away.

When he was finally side by side with the cabin-boy, when he felt the warmth of that curvaceous body, the soft, lukewarm, desired flesh, innocent of any impure contacts, a savage appetite rendered the black man speechless. The lantern-light didn't even reach halfway to the hideaway in which they'd taken refuge. They couldn't even see each other: they felt each other, they sensed each other's presence under the blankets.

After a short, cautious period of silence, Bom-Crioulo, snuggling up close to the boy, whispered something in his ear. Aleixo remained motionless, scarcely even breathing. Curled up, his eyelids instinctively closing with sleep, listening, with one ear pressed against the boards of the deck, to the crash of the waves against the prow, he didn't feel able even to murmur a word. As in a dream, he saw, in succession, the thousand and one promises made by Bom-Crioulo, parading before him: the room on Misericórdia Street in Rio de Janeiro, the theatres, the outings. He remembered the punishment that the black man had suffered for his sake. But he said nothing. A sensation of infinite well-being began to spread through his whole body. He began to feel in his own blood impulses that he had never felt before, a sort of innate desire to give in to the black man's wishes, to let himself go and let the other do whatever he wanted to — a vague relaxation of the nerves, a longing for passiveness.

"Go ahead!" he whispered quickly and rolled over.

And the crime against nature was consummated.

IV

The day had dawned fine and sunny, hot and luminous, with the exquisite transparency of freshly washed crystal.

In the early morning hours, before the last star had faded from the sky, the ship had "stoked its furnaces" and was heading for port now, without using its sails, driven by its obsolete old engine — a practically useless good-for-nothing that puffed out steam and was always breaking down somewhere or other because of its aged machinery.

At last they were arriving!

Now each of the sailors busied himself about his own affairs, his clothes, the things he'd brought from that long trip south, that damned trip that had seemed as if it would never end.

There, right opposite them, to larboard, was the perpendicular cut of the side of Sugar Loaf — dark, steep, wave-lashed, guarding the entrance to the bay; and further away, to the south, the ash-grey peak of Gávea, overlooking the sea — the last ridge of a sort of primitive, rough, inchoate mountain-range.

"And what's that island with the white speck on it?" Aleixo asked, curious.

He was standing beside Bom-Crioulo, raptly contemplating the Rio coastline.

"That's Flat Island," the black man explained. "Don't you see the lighthouse? It's that white thing."

And he began to describe the section of coast which was unfolding itself now to the light, shining and sharply mountainous, the legendary land of the *tamoyos* and *caramurus*.[1] That narrow strip of sand on the other side (and he stretched his arm

---

[1] *Caramura* is the native name of a fish (*Lepidosiren paradoxa*), called in Port. *lampreia* or *moréia*. A shipwrecked Portuguese adventurer, Diogo Alvares, found with eight mates by the Indians in 1509 or 1510, escaped death by being too thin (all the others were eaten). The tribe adopted him and called him *caramuru* because the fish is also long and thin. Also the Portuguese and, later, all the conservative politicians came to be known, in a deprecatory vein, as *caramurus*. *Tamoios* is the name of the tribe which inhabited Rio de Janeiro and surrounding areas.

over the boy's shoulder), by the water's edge, was called Marambaia.[1] Over there, that mountain you could barely see in the distance, was Cabo Frio.[2]

And he continued pointing out, one by one, with patriotic pride, the interesting features of the landscape as they advanced into the bay, and the buildings: the fortress of São João up there on the hill and of Santa Cruz down there by the water, opposite each other, with their silent guns; Red Beach, surrounded by hills; the lunatic asylum; Botafogo.[3]

"And all that over there," he said, with a sweeping gesture that took in hills and houses," all that is the city of Niterói.[4] Have you ever heard of it?"

"No."

"Well, there it is."

As far as that goes, Aleixo was not really experiencing any great surprise. He too had been born among mountains, by the sea. Bom-Crioulo's enthusiasm didn't even stir him. He had a very different idea of what Rio de Janeiro was!

"But this isn't even the city yet, you crazy kid," the black man explained. "You haven't seen anything yet."

The corvette was nearing Villegaignon Island.

Bom-Crioulo had just time enough to say to the cabin-boy: "That's where I began." And he disappeared in the throng of sailors.

It was almost noon. War sloops were approaching the fort, slicing through the water with the smooth rhythm of outriggers. You could hear the synchronised slap of their oars, pacing the rowing.

Around the ferry-boat which went to the beaches other small boats plied back and forth, selling various objects. Launches tooted as they crossed the bay. Warships, motionless, their prows turned toward the mouth of the bay, raised and lowered signal flags. Amongst them was a huge battleship near shore, flat, level and round-bellied, with a blue pennant on its mainmast.

The corvette slowed down, moving forward at a leisurely pace, standing out among all the other ships in the port, with its

---

[1] A long sand-bar which partly closes off Sepetiba Bay, near Rio.

[2] A mountainous cape, and the resort town located on it, some 120 km. northeast of Rio de Janeiro.

[3] A small gulf in Guanabara Bay, located at its southwestern end, behind Sugar Loaf, as well as the adjacent part of the city of Rio.

[4] A residential city located on Guanabara Bay opposite Rio de Janeiro.

air of being some ancient, legendary vessel.

Just before reaching Villegaignon, it made an almost imperceptible stop and gave a slight backwards shunt. There was a great falling noise in the water and then the sound of hawsers unrolling, rushing.

"Thank God!" exclaimed several voices at the same time, as if they'd arranged to combine in a chorus of joy.

Meanwhile, Bom-Crioulo began to feel a twinge of sadness in his soul, a thing that rarely happened to him. He remembered the open seas, his first sighting of Aleixo, the new life he was about to begin, and he worried above all about keeping the cabin-boy's friendship, about the future of that affection which had been born on the trip and which was threatened now by the contingencies of naval service. In less than twenty-four hours Aleixo might be transferred to some other ship — who knows?, he himself, Bom-Crioulo, might not continue serving on the corvette.

Instinctively, his eyes would seek out the boy, alight with a jealous desire to see him always, forever, nearby there, living the same life of work and obedience, growing up at his side like a beloved, inseparable brother.

On the other counts, his mind was at ease, because Aleixo had given him the greatest proof of friendship of all, at a simple nod, a mere look. Wherever they were they would surely always remember that cold night, sleeping under the same blanket in the prow of the corvette, in each other's arms, like a pair of newly-weds in the throes of passion of their first coupling.

At the thought of this, Bom-Crioulo felt an extraordinary fever of eroticism, an uncontrollable ecstasy of homosexual pleasure. Now he understood clearly that only with a man, with a man like himself, could he find what in vain he had looked for among women.

He had never been aware of this anomaly in himself; never in his life did he recall having had to examine his sexual tendencies. Women left him impotent for the act of love, it's true, but it was also impossible for him to imagine, in any way, that sort of vulgar intercourse between individuals of the same sex. And yet — who could have imagined it! — it was happening to him himself now, unexpectedly, with no premeditation on his part. And what was strangest was that "things" threatened to continue this way, as a punishment for his sins, no doubt. Well, there was nothing he could do except be patient, seeing that it was "nature" herself who was imposing this punishment on him.

After all, he was a man, and he had his sexual needs, like any other man. It had been hard enough as it was for him to remain a virgin till the age of thirty, enduring embarrassments that no one would believe, and being obliged often to commit excesses which medical science condemns.[1] Anyhow, his own conscience was clear, all the more so because there were examples right there on board of conduct similar to his — not to mention a certain officer concerning whose personal life terrible rumours were spread. And if the white man did it, the black man was even more likely to! For not everybody has the strength to resist: nature is stronger than the human will.

The job of lowering the ship's boats began, a loud, deafening hurly-burly, the constant noise of ropes and blocks, a confusion of voices and whistles, mingling together in a Babel like that of a public market, which echoed clamorously in the silence of the bay.

All around the corvette swarmed a throng of sloops and launches carrying naval officers and ladies, who waved to the officers on board — the men in "inspection" uniform, with sword and white gloves, putting on an air of authority, standing upright on the back seat of their small vessels with that native agility of men of the sea; the women in summer dress, and very sunburnt.

When the health inspection left, there was a moment of generalised disorder, in which everybody tried to go up the gang-plank, all charging at one and the same time. "Come alongside from there!" one voice cried. "Release the boat!" roared another. "Rowing backwards astern!" "Open up in front!" "Row forwards!"

No one could understand anything in the uproar.

Shortly, however, order began to be restored, the tumult died down, and all that could be heard was the voices of the sailors talking to one another. At that moment a sloop pulled up, flying the English flag, with a blond, bewhiskered officer, who looked very like Kaiser Wilhelm of Germany. He was the captain of the *Ironside*, a British warship.

Austere, buttoned up to the collar, he went up to the captain's quarters and came down again immediately, without even turning to look at anyone, coming down hard on the steps of the

---

[1] These "excesses" are masturbation, which 19th century medicine so violently and puritanically condemned.

staircase.

Bom-Crioulo, who had been leaning over the main rail, muttered to himself, as soon as he saw the Englishman get back on the sloop: "Stupid English fool!" He stood there in his anger, staring into the quiet water. There he was at last, in Guanabara Bay, after six long months' absence. He needed to go ashore that same day to settle the business of the room on Misericórdia Street, before the boy changed his mind; he had things to buy.

But the order was to stay on board, and Bom-Crioulo, like all the rest of the crew, spent a dull, listless afternoon, nodding off with fatigue and drowsiness, occupied with small jobs like cleaning up and elementary manoeuvres. What a hell of a life, with no rest at all! There was hardly time enough for a poor fellow to follow all the orders he got. And if he didn't follow them! It was the pillory, at least, if he wasn't put in chains right away. What a life, what a life! A slave back on the plantation, a slave on board, a slave everywhere. And they called this serving your country!

Night came, a still, starry night, profoundly calm and relaxing. The crew slept a tranquil, untroubled, delightful eight-hour sleep, in the open air, on the rough-hewn deck.

Bom-Crioulo didn't even think about Aleixo. He was hardly able to speak, done in by tiredness, his weak body asking only for physical comfort, his mind and soul in suspense, as it were, his whole being without any desire to do anything whatsoever. He had worked like a draught-horse; he couldn't fight against fatigue any longer. There are times when even animals collapse from sheer exhaustion. He lay down in a corner, far from every-one, and fell right away into a cataleptic sleep. At the first notes of dawn reveille he stretched, yawned, opened his eyes in surprise and felt that he was soaking wet. "Oh!" He ran his hand over the wet area, feeling it, and, making a sickened gesture, found, to his disgust and rage, the irreparable loss he had unconsciously suffered while he was asleep. He had had a real outpouring of seminal liquid, of procreative strength, of life, in short, because "that juice" was blood transformed into living matter! If he'd even enjoyed it, at the very least. But he hadn't felt anything, anything at all, not even in a dream! He had slept all night like a stupid animal, and the result was there on the sheet — almost a river of life-giving semen![1]

---

[1] There was — and is — in Latin America a generalized belief that the loss of semen gravely debilitated a man. Thus Bom-Crioulo's anger at his nocturnal emission.

Sad and despairing, cursing nature in the rough language of the galley-slave, he got up and set about folding his bedclothing, brusquely, violently, as if someone else had contributed to his "misfortune".

He started the day out like someone with a chip on his shoulder. His face wore a dour expression of annoyance; he spoke little and roughly, threateningly, telling his comrades to leave him be, to leave him in peace, he was in no mood for jokes, watch out or he'd split somebody's head open!

The other sailors humbly begged his pardon and tried to flatter and appease him, because they knew that "that nigger is half-crazy".

In the afternoon, however, his nerves settled down, thanks to Aleixo, who had gone and asked him, with a certain amount of self-interest and with a tone of meekness in his adolescent voice, if he was ready to go ashore.

"Why not? They've given us shore leave."

"Ah! I thought you'd forgotten."

"What d'you mean, forgotten? Didn't I tell you that we were going to make arrangements for our little nest this very day?"

And he added affectionately:

"I hope to God we'll be able to sleep there for the first time tonight."

But the cabin-boy hadn't been given leave yet. Aleixo didn't have the courage to ask to be allowed to go ashore; he was afraid the answer would be no. Bom-Crioulo tried to encourage him, told him not to be crazy, suggested that he ask to be allowed to go ashore for just a minute and then come back, or that he think up some excuse for going.

"Tell the first mate you have a rich relative in Rio, or something like that."

Aleixo finally got up nerve, and, shortly afterwards, came back very pleased with himself, smiling, hopscotching along.

"There's nothing in the world like being a pretty boy. Even the officers like you."

But Bom-Crioulo didn't like the joke. He fixed his eyes on the lad as if he were going to launch a thunderbolt against him: "hmm! hmm!" he muttered. But the cabin-boy corrected himself quickly: "It was a joke, Bom-Crioulo, just a joke. Can't I even make a joke?"

"Things like that aren't jokes," the black man replied. "When I like somebody I really like them, and that's that! I've already told you to watch your step."

They dressed for shore and set out in the five o'clock sloop, after evening meal.

"First we'll have a shot of rum," said Bom-Crioulo as they got out on the Pharoux dock. "Right here in this stall. You have to warm up the kidneys a bit."

"I don't want any."

"You have to drink at least a glass of *maduro*."[1]

"What's *maduro*?"

"It's a very nice drink."

And they walked on.

The clock on the tower of the ferry-boat terminal marked a quarter to six, and the city, submerged in twilight, was slowly going to sleep, was falling little by little into the apathy of an abandoned square, into the melancholy stillness of a distant village.

Lights went on, and passers-by became fewer and fewer in the Palace Square. Only a few groups of stragglers were left, standing around in the darkness, as well as people who got off the trolleys, clutching packages, opposite the ferry-boat terminal. The decaying old abode of the Braganças,[2] the sombre palace from which, for almost a century, the monarchy extorted money from the people, sat in mournful immobility, solitary and closed at that hour.

Bom-Crioulo turned to the left under the palace bridge and went up Misericórdia Street, arm in arm with the cabin-boy, smoking a cigar he'd bought at a stall in the square.

Further up, near the War Arsenal, they stopped in front of a two-story house with shuttered windows. It was a very ancient-looking house, with two worm-eaten wooden balconies on the second floor and, up above, on the roof, a sort of attic, hidden, buried, almost hanging suspended. Underneath, on the ground floor, lived a family of Negroes from Angola. You could hear, at that moment, the shouts of the blacks in the dark interior of that African hideout.

"Here we are," said Bom-Crioulo, recognising the house; he disappeared into the unlighted corridor that led to the second floor. Aleixo accompanied him in silence, without a word, keeping close to the wall, like someone entering an unfamiliar place for the first time.

"Come on, you crazy kid!" said the black man, taking his arm. "What are you afraid of?"

---

[1] A fermented drink made of sugar, sugar-water or molasses, mixed with water.

[2] The family name of the Portuguese and Brazilian royal family. The palace referred to here, the former Brazilian royal palace, is at present the Post and Telegraph Office, in 15th of November Square.

They climbed the staircase carefully, a sad, unused staircase, whose steep steps seemed at any moment about to vanish under their feet.

The black man pulled the rope hanging from the grilled door, and, inside, in the dining-room, a bell responded, tinkling dully.

No one came.

Bom-Crioulo pulled again, harder.

"Who's there? Oh!..."

"It's me, Miz Carolina. Be so kind as to open up."

"I'm coming."

And in a minute the sailor threw himself into the arms of a round, chubby, middle-aged woman, pressing her to his chest, even lifting her off the ground, despite her weight, with the spontaneous happiness of friends who meet again, after a long absence.

"Tell me all about it, Bom-Crioulo, come on, come in. Who's this young lad?"

"This young lad? Well, that's why I'm here. We'll talk about that later."

"And how are *you*, my fine black buck? Tell me, tell me everything. If I'd known it was you at the door. Come on, give me another hug!"

And they hugged each other again, breathlessly, chuckling and laughing. Miz Carolina wore an apron and was quite pudgy. Her hair was braided in two tresses and parted down the middle. Bom-Crioulo was using all his charm, showering her with compliments, telling her she looked plumper, prettier, younger than ever!

Miz Carolina was a Portuguese lady who rented out rooms on Misericórdia Street, but only to people of a certain "type", people who didn't put on airs or make pretensions to elegance, yet people whom she knew and trusted nevertheless, good tenants, Portuguese from her own country, old friends. Race and colour meant nothing to her, nor did the social class or profession of her lodger. Sailor, soldier, seafarer, bartender — they were all the same to her, and she treated all alike, with equal amiability.

She earned her living from her house, from her rooms, renting them out by the month or by the hour. She had her man — why should she deny that? But, besides him, and any other "affairs" she might have, she had to make a living from something more solid, something more or less profitable that could provide for her future. Because you can't count on men: they're here today and gone tomorrow.

When she was a young girl, when she was twenty, she'd opened up her own house on Lampadosa Street. Those were the days! Money poured in that door like morning sunlight, without her even having to worry about it. A fortune in jewels, gold and diamonds! She was already plump, even then: they called her Big-Ass Carole, a vulgar nickname, invented by the *hoi polloi*.

Then she fell very sick. Sores broke out all over her body, and she thought she wasn't going to survive. Everything is transitory in this life: she was never able to pull herself up again. In her time of misfortune, she even had to pawn her jewels and everything she owned, because nobody sought her out, nobody wanted her. She was a poor street bitch without an owner. She went through the hardest times! She even wanted to enter the theatre, in any role, even working as a servant-girl. And it was about that time, one day during carnival (well she remembered!), that her luck began to change. A small club paid her a few *mil-réis* to act the role of Venus in an allegorical float, in the parade. She was a *succès de scandale*: people threw her flowers, they cheered, they applauded, they gave her presents — good Lord! For nearly a year the main topic of discussion in Rio was Carolina, the legs of Carolina, that Portuguese girl on Núncio Street.

The poor woman would tell this story with tears in her eyes and signs of deep, painful nostalgia, as she repeated: "Those were the days! Those were the days!"

She was the mistress of two men, she fell sick again, she went back to Portugal, she returned to Brazil cured and plump and full of new ambitions, she lived with another man, and, finally, after a life of many pleasures and much suffering, here she was, on Misericórdia Street, trying to keep alive, my dear!, exploiting the worst instincts of the rotten human race, while her "man" was involved in deals concerning fresh meat and the furnishing of supplies to military barracks.[1]

This union with the butcher, Mr. Brás, a man with a bushy

---

[1] The suggestion here definitely is that, just as Miz Carolina is engaged in clandestine activities involving prostitution, her "man" is supplying meat that is not "fresh", or comes from illegal abattoirs, or is supplied in insufficient quantities, according to contract stipulations, or some other way infringes legal dispositions. The supplying of military barracks has always been a coveted source of illicit enrichment in Brazil.

beard and many possessions, really brought little or no profit to Miz Carolina, because he was married, and only once a month did he remember her, giving her the miserable sum of one-hundred-and-fifty *mil-réis* to pay the rent on the house — besides the meat, which he sent every day.

"I have forty years of experience," she would say, "forty years and a few silver threads on this head of mine. I know this old world, my dear, and in my opinion it's all misery and suffering."

She had admired Bom-Crioulo since the day when he, quite unselfishly, by a providential accident, saved her from being stabbed to death by thieves. She would have been willing to get down and kiss the sailor's feet, because she had never seen such courage and such unselfishness!

Miz Carolina always sought an opportunity to recall the incident, narrating it in full colour, even lending it certain Rembrantian hues, gushing praise of the navy, lauding seamen as "benefactors of humanity".

One night — just thinking about it made her shiver! — she was returning from a performance of *Drama on the High Seas*, which was playing at the Phoenix Theatre,[1] when, just as she was inserting the key into the lock of her door, she was caught in the act by two individuals, whose features she couldn't recognise. They demanded she give them her rings and all the cash she had on her.

And, as a matter of fact, besides a diamond ring (a souvenir of the good old days!) and two emeralds, she had fifty *mil-réis* in her possession. It was after midnight, and Misericórdia Street was lonelier than a cemetery. And no police or guards anywhere around! She thought of shouting for help, but the brigands reminded her that, if she dared to shout, they'd kill her. And they threatened her with their knives, two fine steel blades, the size of butcher-knives! Ah, but God watches over His children! At that very moment she saw a sailor passing, and she rushed toward him, shouting "Help! Help!" A fight ensued. The sailor leapt and jumped around, avoiding the thieves' knives, and then attacking, like a wild animal, with his own pocket-knife in hand. Fortunately (God works in a mysterious way!), at her cries of distress, the windows of the neighbouring houses filled with people in night shirts, whistles were blown in the darkness, and the police arrived in time to catch the thieves, who had been

---

[1] One of the oldest, most elaborately decorated and most famous of the theatres of Rio de Janeiro, located on Rua da Carioca (Carioca Street). Still standing, it is now a movie theatre.

completely disarmed by the providential sailor. Anybody else in her position would have done what she did. She opened a bottle of beer for her saviour, who said that his name was Amaro, and his nickname Bom-Crioulo, and that he was a sailor on a ship of the Brazilian fleet. And since sailors from on board lived in her rooming-house, Bom-Crioulo became well-known there, and an intimacy grew up immediately between Miz Carolina and the black man. On her word of honour, she'd never seen so brave a man!

She admired him for that, because he was a courageous sailor — man enough to take on four!

Bom-Crioulo began to frequent her house, which other sailors also visited, and that's how the great affection that Miz Carolina had for him began. She had no ulterior motives: she knew that the black man was not the kind who is interested in women.

"Come on, now, tell me all about that trip!"

All three had sat down in the dining-room, in the gas-light. Miz Carolina, heat-smitten, very plump, shaking her head, breathless, was eager to hear news. The black man, his sailor's cap atop his head, leaning back familiarly, was finishing his cigar, whose tip lighted up now and then in a hot, red glow. Aleixo, motionless in his chair, looked at the walls, examining the wallpaper and the pictures there — cheap, inferior copies of oil-paintings, dealing with *boudoir* themes, placed symmetrically, two on each wall — the almost empty china-cabinet, and a collection of matchbox seals arranged in the shape of a fan. Everything was old and discoloured, dusty and shabby. The air was heavy with camphor and cooking-grease, ventilated only by a sad little window that opened onto a sort of yard on the ground floor.

Bom-Crioulo summed up the corvette's trip in a few words: "Six months of routine and boredom! Only Aleixo cheered things up a little bit, on the return trip."

And he launched into the story of the cabin-boy.

"Now Miz Carolina is going to fix a room up for us, even if it's on the roof," he wound up. "Just a little room without any frills, for when we come ashore."

"One bed or two?" asked the landlady, with a smile.

"As you wish. Sailors are people who can sleep four, five, fifty to a bed! If you had a wide single bed..."

"I'll find one, good Lord, I'll find one," Miz Carolina replied. "The room up on top is vacant, and, d'you know?, I think you'd like it better up there."

Smilingly, slyly, suffocated by the heat, she winked at Bom-Crioulo.

"Well, I can see that you've come back a different man. That was a lucky trip! It must have been the sea or what they call Spanish fly!"

They laughed, in mutual understanding, while Aleixo, leaning over the windowsill, spat into the yard of the African quarters below.

V

From the very first night he slept in the upstairs room, Bom-Crioulo began to feel a special, intimate pleasure, as well as a sort of solitary spiritual joy — a certain love for the obscure life of that house which of late almost no one visited and which was his beloved refuge, the refuge of the sailor resting from his labours, the sweet repose of his voluptuous soul. He couldn't imagine a better life, a more ideal, comfortable shelter. The world was now summed up for him in this: a little room under the eaves, Aleixo and. . .nothing more! As long as God kept him in sound mind and good health, there was nothing else he wanted.

The room was separate from the rest of the house, with a window looking down into the yard. It was a sort of attic, termite-riddled and stinking of carbolic acid. [1] A young Portugese immigrant who had recently arrived had died there of yellow fever. But though Bom-Crioulo feared the more dangerous fevers, he paid no attention to this fact; he tried to forget the matter and settled in once and for all. All the money he could lay his hands on went to buy furniture and fancy little rococo objects, figurines, decorations, things of no value, often brought from on board ship. Little by little the tiny room acquired the appearance of a Jewish bazaar, as it filled up with bric-à-brac, and accumulated empty boxes, vulgar sea-shells and other ornamental accessories. The bed was an already much used folding canvas one, over which Bom-Crioulo carefully spread a thick red blanket every morning, when he got up, "to hide the stains."

For months he led a peaceful life, scrupulously regulated, rigorously methodical, fulfilling his duties on board, coming ashore twice a week with Aleixo, without giving any cause for punishments or scoldings. Even the officers were surprised at his behaviour and wondered at his new ways.

---

[1] Carbolic acid (phenol, phenic acid, phenyl alcohol), because of its powerful antiseptic qualities and penetrating odour, was much used at the time as a disinfectant.

"This is only temporary," suggested Lieutenant Sousa. "Soon we'll have him here again, drunk and raising hell. For as long as I've known him, he's always been a rebel against any of the rules of normal living. One day he's meek as a lamb, the next, wild as a lion. It's the African temperament."

As for the cabin-boy, his soul was bathed in the perpetual cheerfulness of those lucky people who don't have a care in the world. Ashore or aboard, he had nothing to complain about. He was always neat and clean; no one ever saw him lying around on deck or getting his clothes dirty with tar up in the prow. Fortunately, the first mate, recognising that he was a well-behaved, clean, obedient, hard-working boy, had chosen him for the duties of chief cabin-boy, as a reward for his good conduct. As a result, Aleixo was seldom amongst the other sailors. His favourite spot was up on the bridge, or astern, sewing flags, cutting out pennants, and learning various of the requirements of his job. Sometimes he would talk with the officer on watch, telling stories of Santa Catarina, anecdotes about his state, about the days when he was just a fisherman's son, just a poor boy living by the sea. There was a midshipman, a very well-brought-up, democratic young chap, who once in a while would give him money, loose change to buy cigarettes with. Then he'd go running to Bom-Crioulo to show him the *tostões*[1] that "my midshipman gave me." Everybody on board petted him and spoiled him; even Agostinho the guard, harsh and brusque, treated him kindly, with a soft tone in his voice when he addressed him. The good life!

As for when he was ashore, in the room on Misericórdia Street, why even mention that? There he led the life of a prince! He and the black man would sit around in their undershorts and tumble about as they pleased on the old canvas bed (which was very cool in hot weather), with the bottle of white rum standing by, by themselves there, absolutely free and independent, laughing and chatting at ease, without anyone ever coming to disturb them, with the door locked just as an extra precaution.

Only one thing vexed the cabin-boy — the black man's sexual whims. Because Bom-Crioulo was not satisfied merely with possessing him sexually at any hour of the day or night. He wanted much more; he obliged the boy to go to extremes, he made a slave, a whore of him, suggesting to him that they perform every extravagant act that came into his mind. The very

---

[1]Plural of *tostão*, a former Brazilian coin, worth 100 reis. (see p. 53, note 3.)

first night he wanted Aleixo to strip, to strip right down to the buff: he wanted to see his body.

Aleixo replied sulkily that that wasn't something you asked a man to do! Anything but *that*. But the black man insisted. Nobody was going to change his mind or take that desire away from him: "Either we're friends or we're not."

"What nonsense!" said the boy. Stripping right down in Bom-Crioulo's presence. He knew that he was ashamed to do that.

"Ashamed of what?" replied the black man. "Where did this 'shame' come from? Aren't you a man like me?"

"Of course I am!"

"Then stop being so fussy, kid; come on, take off your clothes."

There was light in the room, a pale, dying light, from the wick of a tallow candle.

"You can't even see anything," whimpered Aleixo tearlessly.

"You can always see something."

And the boy, obedient and afraid, slowly unbuttoned his flannel shirt and then his trousers. He was standing, and he placed his clothes on the bed, item by item.

Bom-Crioulo's desire was satisfied. Aleixo appeared before him now in full, exuberant nudity, his skin very white, his curvaceous buttocks standing out in the voluptuous semi-darkness of the room, in the caressing half-shade of that unknown and shameless sanctuary of passions that may not be mentioned. He was a lovely model of male adolescence, such as the Greece of Venus would perhaps immortalise in stanzas of limpid gold and statues of a sculpture both powerful and sensual. Sodom was reborn in a sad, desolate hovel on Misericórdia Street, which at that hour was submerged in the sweet tranquility of an isolated hermitage.

"Look and get it over with," mumbled the boy, steadying his feet.

Bom-Crioulo was in ecstasy! The solid, milky whiteness of that tender flesh made his whole body tremble, affecting his nerves in a strange way, exciting him like strong drink, attracting him, stirring his heart. He had never seen such a beautifully rounded male body, such arms, such firm, fleshy hips. With breasts, Aleixo would be a real woman! What a marvellous neck, what delightful shoulders — it was enough to drive a man crazy!

All the raging desire of the bull when he senses the presence of the female roared within the black man. His whole being was shaken, tarrying over that sensual nudity in pagan idolatry like a worshipper before a gold ikon or an artist in the presence of a masterpiece. Ignorant and coarse, he nevertheless felt moved to his very innermost roots, to the depths of his moral and physical nature; he felt himself dominated by an almost blind respect for the cabin-boy, who, in his eyes, the eyes of a mere crude sailor, attained the proportions of a supernatural being.

"That's enough!" implored Aleixo.

"No, no! Just a little longer."

Bom-Crioulo took up the candle, trembling, and, coming closer, continued his detailed examination of the cabin-boy, feeling his flesh, praising the perfume of his skin, at the peak of lustfulness, at the extremity of desire, his eyes darting sparks of pleasure.

"That's all!" said Aleixo suddenly, impatient by now, and blew out the candle.

There followed then, in the darkness, a slight skirmish of whispered words and groans. And when Bom-Crioulo, once more triumphant, lit a match, he could hardly stand on his own two feet.

These were the "vexations" that Aleixo had to bear. Apart from that, his life flowed along smoothly, like a light pleasure-craft blown by favourable winds.

Miz Carolina gave him the affectionate nickname of "bitty pretty boy." "My bitty pretty boy," as she said, softening her Portuguese accent.

She found him infinitely delightful, that little mannikin dressed up as a sailor, blond and white-skinned, always with his silky hair well combed, and his boots polished and shiny, smelling of perfume, like a young girl who's becoming a woman.

The boy, very susceptible to any kind of affection, was grateful to her, and he never went up to the room without first greeting Miz Carolina, sharing innocent confidences with her, letting her spoil and flatter him.

He, Miz Carolina and Bom-Crioulo were like a little family. They had no secrets from one another, and they loved one another, mutually.

What more could he ask for from life? Far from his parents, in a strange land, he found in that house on Misericórdia Street a loving shelter, a paradise of happiness.

A few days after arriving in Rio de Janeiro, the corvette went into dry dock.

As soon as that great basin of granite, wide and deep, like

some abyss sculpted by nature, that had been opened up with pickaxes in the hard, implacable bosom of the rock, had been drained of its water, the work began.

A continuous, Cyclopean hammering resounded in the interior of that stone sepulchre, as though in some subterranean forge. Workers in shirtsleeves began anew every day the same brutal task of caulking the belly of the old "wreck," while the sailors, in another spot, went around scraping off the mussels, which were rotting in the heat of the dry bottom of the dock. The strong smell of decomposing shellfish was suffocating down there; it came up like waves of odour from a dunghill and even the application of potash and carbolic acid wasn't sufficient to get rid of it.

And it was December, a month of epidemics and unbearable heat.

You would almost have thought that the men there, workmen and sailors alike, had no respiratory tract, or no lungs, or that they were simply saturated with those foul emanations.

They sang as they worked, and they whistled as they hammered away, heroically indifferent, without thinking about the great risks they were running.

But at night, from sunset on, the pestilential odour would grow stronger and stronger, and then there was no alternative. All the sailors would rush out of the dry dock like an excited anthill, holding their noses and shouting: "Get out! Get out! Yellow fever!"[1]

Ship in dry dock, sailor at liberty. Ship's work diminished; there was more freedom; you could laze around as you wished, because there was plenty of opportunity: living quarters stretched for a certain distance over the surface of the island. From there the shore was only a hop, skip and jump away, and there were always boats for hire waiting. A large number of dinghies selling provisions moored near the dry dock; and life went on just as it would have gone on anywhere else.

Now and then: "Lieutenant, may I have permission to go visit a friend in naval hospital?"

"You can go, but don't stay too long."

The hospital was on the highest point of the island, on a hill reached by a zigzag path. Every afternoon, sailors went by in

---

[1]At the time of the writing of this novel, the cause of yellow fever — very prevalent in Rio de Janeiro — had not been identified as the *anopheles* mosquito; it was thought to be caused by marshes, "miasmas", etc.

that direction, climbing slowly in groups of four, as if in procession. They were going to visit friends in hospital, or they were new patients coming in from the fleet.

Bom-Crioulo redoubled his visits ashore now. He was diligent in performing his duties; he never refused to do what he was ordered to; he fulfilled his obligations as patiently as in former times, when the future still smiled on him with promises of a better life. He was clearly rehabilitating his reputation, which had suffered from various of his antics and actions while travelling on the high seas. The first mate gave him many special privileges, but he warned him "to be careful, not to drink too much."

The first mate was a friend, a real father to every hard-working, law-abiding sailor; all that you had to do to be in his good graces was to be an honest fellow and behave properly.

Bom-Crioulo understood this, and did everything in his power not to displease him. He worked whenever there was work to be done, with a happy smile, without any compulsion, knowing full well that he would be able to go ashore when he wanted to.

Every second day would find him there in his room on Misericórdia Street, given over totally to relaxation, free, utterly free of problems and duties.

He never neglected to drink his shot of "Brazilian cognac," but he knew how to control himself and avoid drinking too much. Besides, his life was so calm, it flowed so smoothly, so sweetly, that he himself was really surprised.

Lately, he'd begun to imagine that he was getting thin, and he had even felt a few twinges of weakness in his chest.[1] When he worked very hard or made any kind of special effort, a deep drowsiness would settle on him, a desire to stretch his bones out on a cool, soft bed, a sort of slackness of the nerves. Even his fellow-sailors noticed a certain change in his physical appearance: "You're thin, Bom-Crioulo, what the hell's wrong?"

"Me, thin?" And he'd run his hand over his face, feeling himself. Could it be some disease?

"Some pretty nigger gal, eh?"

"To hell with nigger gals!"

One day he asked the cabin-boy:

"D'you think I'm getting thinner?"

Aleixo also thought so, but said it was "not very noticeable".

---

[1] The references to Bom-Crioulo's growing thinness are evidence of the 19th century belief in the deleterious effects of sexual intercourse or loss of semen in any form.

Bom-Crioulo didn't worry. He kept on living calmly, on board and ashore, enjoying a profound peace of mind, watching Aleixo grow up at his side, witnessing the premature development of certain organs in him, the blossoming of the second age, like someone studying the evolution of some rare flower.

His friendship for the cabin-boy was no longer a burning, lascivious relationship. It had changed into a calm sentiment, a mutual affection, without the feverish impulses or the jealousy of the impassioned lover.

Almost a year of living together had been sufficient for him to be able to identify completely with the cabin-boy, to get to know him as he really was, and he had the conviction that Aleixo would not be untrue to him, would not surrender to the male fury of just any brute who came along. All this, and the certainty that the boy respected him, gave him that confident peacefulness characteristic of the happy husband, of the zealous capitalist who has his money placed, safe from all dangers.

Almost a year had gone by, and the tough thread of that mysterious friendship, nurtured in an attic at the top of Misericórdia Street, had not been subject to the slightest tension. The two sailors lived for each other; they complemented each other.

"You two are going to end up having children," Miz Carolina would joke.

She said she had never seen two men who liked each other so much! Bom-Crioulo wasn't crazy or anything near it. The crazy one was the person who thought he was crazy.

And the black man would smile proudly, showing his ivory-white teeth, slightly pointed, like sharks' teeth.

The corvette finally left dry dock and tied up at a buoy behind St. Benedict's Hill,[1] opposite the Navy Arsenal.

That was nearer land, anyhow, than being in the "pit", where the warships anchored, where you had no freedom at all.

But one day Bom-Crioulo was taken by surprise by the news that he had been transferred to another ship — a steel battleship, famous for its complicated machinery and its impressive artillery capacity: a superb blend of naval advantages, which made that ship one of the most powerful in the world.

Bom-Crioulo was angry. Sons of bitches! A man didn't even have time to get to know a ship any more, serving on one today, on another tomorrow. It must be a joke!

And raging, tying his canvas bag, he said sullenly:

---

[1] A small hill near the dock area in downtown Rio de Janeiro, on top of which the Benedictine monastery (São Bento) is located.

"That's what a sailor gets for lowering his guard; that's what he gets."

While the other sailors strolled back and forth from stern to prow, calmly, at ease, he was going to be sent to the battleship, just because he was a good sailor — to that steel devil, to that monster, without Aleixo, without his Aleixo. He had lived for so many months there aboard the corvette with the boy, and now, suddenly, without rime or reason: transferred. It was really a crime!

But God's ways are not our ways! thought Bom-Crioulo. God knows what he's doing, and human beings just have to obey in silence, because a sailor and a black slave — in the long run, they come down to the same thing.

Aleixo, resigned to the transfer, tried to console him: "Be patient, man, it isn't the end of the world. We'll still see each other, what the hell!" That's why they'd rented the room. Every second day they could meet ashore just as before.

"Now you'll have to watch your step," warned the black man.

All his jealousy came alive again. That sudden, unexpected separation irritated him, awakening in the depths of his soul an exacerbated egotism, a vague lack of confidence in the future. It's true the cabin-boy was no longer a baby who could be easily deluded by anybody, but, my dear friend, the boy might very well become infatuated with some handsome young officer, and then, goodbye, Bom-Crioulo!

His spirit heavy with apprehension, with sad eyes and a gloomy expression on his face, he embraced his beloved Aleixo. Without saying a word more, mute in his sorrow, like a prisoner leaving one prison to enter another, he watched the masts of the corvette disappear, and, along with them, the silhouette of the cabin-boy, who waved to him from afar off now, in the half-light of dusk, vague and nebulous, like the very spirit of nostalgia.

The warship was hidden behind the island, huge and solemn, with its noble air of a floating fortress, prow pointed seawards, honourable and glorious.

"Row hard, it's late!"

And the little sloop, moving vigorously forward, was leaving behind, without knowing it, the soul of Bom-Crioulo, tender and suffering.

VI

The next day Aleixo found the door of the room closed. So, Bom-Crioulo had not come ashore, as he'd promised. He must be on duty, thought the boy. For naval discipline was a very different thing on the battleship. There, the first mate, a violent individual, did nothing but talk of canings and the pillory. He was very glad to stay on his corvette, even if it was old and run-down.

He opened the window to let the light in and began to undress, singing to himself, his gaze lost in the motionless air outside, in the flashing blue of the sky. The heat was infernal. Not even a breeze. Torrential and triumphant, the rays of the two o'clock sun fell obliquely on the house, gilding the roof-tiles, dusting the windowpanes with shining yellow jewels. An unimaginable profusion of light!

Aleixo undressed, lit up a cigarette for the first time and stretched out at his ease on the old canvas bed. Lord! What an oven!

He wanted to rest awhile, to wait for Bom-Crioulo till five o'clock, to take a nap. He'd left ship quite early because he'd made a date with the black man; and now the only thing to do was wait, in this dizzying heat. Anyhow, he'd see if he could sleep; he'd been on watch the night before.

He didn't even finish the cigarette, a vile thing made of cheap, strong tobacco that Bom-Crioulo had left on the table and that spilled open completely in his clumsy hands. He didn't understand what the devil pleasure smokers got out of smoking. Ugh! *He* certainly wasn't getting used to the smoke. It gave him a headache right off.

He started to look at the roof, the walls, a portrait of the Emperor, now very faded, which he had once seen on the front page of an illustrated newspaper, set in a bamboo frame, an illustrated wall-calendar. He examined the little room and the furniture — a table and two chairs — intently, as if he were in a museum full of rare objects.

He fell asleep just as Miz Carolina's clock, downstairs on the second floor, struck two o'clock.

He woke up startled, feeling out of sorts, bathed in sweat, his tongue dry — stretching and yawning as though he'd slept all night.

The sun was a little less fierce, and there were clouds now up in the sky, breaking the monotony of blue. It was useless. Bom-Crioulo certainly wasn't going to show up now, the cabin-boy thought. What a bore!

As far as that went, he really didn't miss the black man that much. He liked him, of course, but his absence wasn't an open wound that would never heal.

He entertained this idea like a happy memory, like some strange fluid that had been injected into his blood. Maybe he could meet some wealthy man, someone who was somebody. He was already accustomed to doing "those things" by now. Bom-Crioulo himself had told him that nobody pays attention to things like that in Rio de Janeiro. After all, what could he hope for from Bom-Crioulo? Nothing, and, meanwhile, he was sacrificing his health, his body, his youth. It just wasn't worth it!

He jumped out of bed and began dressing slowly, whistling softly, his mind absorbed by that idea. He was bored, really bored with it all; he needed to change his whole way of life.

"May I come in?"

"Oh! ma'am . . ."

It was Miz Carolina. She hadn't seen her "bitty pretty boy" yet, and she was lonesome for him.

"Didn't Bom-Crioulo come today?"

No, he hadn't come. And Aleixo told the story of the black man's transfer to the battleship, of Bom-Crioulo's unhappiness, of the hard life of labour he was going to lead on the other ship.

"Poor Bom-Crioulo!" mourned Miz Carolina. "But he'll surely come ashore."

"Yes, of course, he'll have to come ashore. It won't be so often as on the corvette."

"Poor chap!"

"There's a chair over there," suggested Aleixo. "Why don't you sit down?"

"It's so hot, isn't it?" said the woman, as she took a seat. "We're going to have rain."

And then, with intense curiosity, she added:

"Are you going out?"

"Yes, I'm going to take a walk. I spent such a boring day."

"You miss the nigger, don't you?" emphasised the landlady, underlining her meaning with a smile, as she fanned herself with her apron.

She had sat down, red as a beet, her dress gathered up, bare-foot in a pair of cloth-covered wooden clogs she used when she washed clothes out in the yard.

"No," said Aleixo, with a touch of disdain in his voice. "I was already getting tired of that."

"Already? That's rather soon, my friend."

And she continued, in a fraternal tone:

"Well, he has a good heart, poor fellow. Sometimes I feel sorry for him."

"That's because you don't really know him, ma'am. Yes, he has a good heart, but when he gets angry, God help us! He even frightens me."

"Really?"

"I'm telling you, ma'am!"

"Well, my boy, let me tell you I've never seen Bom-Crioulo angry."

"He's like a wild animal!"

Aleixo was in front of the mirror, putting the finishing touches to his *toilette*. His hair, dripping with oil, sleek and smooth, had the fleeting sheen of dark silk. He parted it to one side and combed it down the left side of his forehead, almost to the eyebrow. That was one of his principal concerns — to have his hair always well-oiled, well-combed. And it was such a lot of work to get it right! He started over again an endless number of times, putting it in order once more, and, finally, after repeated attempts, he put his cap on, slowly and elegantly.

"Ready!" he said, giving the last touch to it.

"That's the way I like to see a sailor," said the woman, flat-teringly, getting up to straighten his shirt-collar, which was doubled over. "I don't like to have anything to do with dirty men."

And, standing in front of Aleixo, with her elbows arched out and hands on her hips:

"You're a real charmer, you little devil! Now I'll bet you're going to go courting some strumpet in Rocio Square!"

The adolescent gave a rather forced laugh, as he looked at himself in the mirror one last time.

"What d'you mean, ma'am? From here I'm going straight to the Passeio Público. I'll be back here at nine o'clock, at the latest."

"And you aren't going to invite me to come along?"

"If you want to come, let's go."

"No, thank you very much. Enjoy yourself and come straight back here; that's all I want."

They were leaving the room.

"But listen," said Miz Carolina resolutely, at the head of the stairs. "I have to talk to you, so come back early."

"Why don't you talk to me now?"

"No, no. When you get back. I'd rather be able to chat comfortably."

"Fine. I'll be back in a jiffy. See you then!"

"See you then."

And in a loud voice, from the top of the stairs, as the cabin-boy disappeared in the hallway, she said:

"Take care, eh?"

It was getting dark; it must have been a little after six. The streetlamps were already on. The heat persisted — a sultry, subterranean atmosphere, oxygenless, heavy and asphyxiating.

The landlady went down the attic stairs, which creaked under her weight, and went to light the gas in the dining-room. She was in a very good mood, and she sang a song from her homeland, in a languid, tremulous voice.

Some days before, a rather extravagant idea had entered her head. She had decided to seduce Aleixo, the "bitty pretty boy", to take him for her own, to have him as the young lover of her old, worn heart, to be his mistress in secret and give him whatever he needed — clothes, shoes, meals on his days off — to give him everything, in short.

It was a whim like any other whim. She was tired of putting up with rough, coarse older men. Now she wanted to try a young boy, a beardless youth, who would obey all her orders. And no one was better for the rôle than Aleixo, whose beauty had impressed her from the first time she saw him. Aleixo was perfect for the rôle: handsome, strong, perhaps still a virgin.

It could be arranged quite easily, without Bom-Crioulo's knowledge. But how was she going to broach the subject to the cabin-boy, how was she going to propose the matter to him? He might be offended; there might even be a scandal.

The best thing to do would be to let him know little by little how much she liked him, offering herself little by little, stimulating him.

Other women older than she was bragged of their conquests; why shouldn't she, who was only thirty-eight years old, have the right to her pleasure too? Too old? Nonsense! Women are always women and men are always men.

She looked at herself in the mirror, and she saw that she really still would "do". What d'you mean, old? Not a wrinkle, not a crow's foot — was that what being old meant? Of course not.

Nobody cared about a person's age. What mattered was the face and the body. What nonsense!

She began to behave very sweetly toward the boy, keeping candies and other dainties for him, ironing his kerchiefs with her own hand, praising him in the presence of third parties, pretending not to be aware of what she was doing when she wanted to show him the richness of her bodily attributes — legs, arms or breasts. On one occasion Aleixo saw her lying on her bed in a short slip, with her legs sticking out; because her bedroom opened on the hallway, and that day she had forgotten to close the door. The cabin-boy averted his gaze quickly, very respectfully, as if he had profaned something. But later, when he remembered the incident, he always felt little thrills of pleasure; he couldn't suppress a sensation of weakness, a kind of faintness, along with an erection caused by his nervous excitement.

He had never forgotten that bedroom scene: a woman lying down, showing her very plump, downy legs — in an irresistible state of disorder, her arms bare, her hair flowing free. It must be marvellous to sleep in the arms of a woman, he thought. And the Portuguese landlady was really not so bad-looking.

But Aleixo was far from imagining that Miz Carolina, that same kindly, gentle Miz Carolina who treated him like her son, wanted to make him her lover.

Such an idea had never passed through his head. He saw men go into her room; he knew of her affair with the butcher. But these were all things she did with other adults. What seemed impossible to him, what he didn't even imagine, was that Miz Carolina could be interested in a young boy his age, almost a baby.

"Here I am!" he said, on his return from the Passeio Público.

"Oh! You're back soon!" exclaimed the landlady, getting up. "Come in here, my bedroom's cooler."

Miz Carolina's bedroom was right under the attic, at the front of the house, a spacious spinster's bedroom, in the middle of which stood a fine double bed with lace pillows.

When the cabin-boy arrived, she was in the dining-room, reading the advertisements in the *Jornal do Comércio*, by the gas light.

"Did you have a good time?"

"A good time? I just went and came back again."

"Because of me?"

"No, the Passeio was dull today. Hardly any people."

Aleixo stopped at the threshold of the room as though he were afraid to go in.

"Come in, my boy, come in, this room is ours, it's the room of your old Portuguese landlady, can't you see?"

And, more cheerful than he'd ever seen her before, she went around joyfully opening the windows that looked out on Misericórdia Street.

While the boy had been out, she had fixed herself up. She had combed her hair, changed her clothes, replaced the clogs with a pair of scarlet high-heeled shoes, and put on her rings, the famous rings that the thieves had tried to take from her: she was completely transformed.

"Sit down, don't be silly, my boy!"

Aleixo sat down, very bashfully, with the air of a high-school boy entering a brothel for the first time. He'd been living in that house for a year now, and this was the first time he had gone in there, into the landlady's bedroom.

"What a lovely room!"

"What d'you mean, lovely, my boy? You're joking, aren't you?" said the woman as she lighted the gas, laughing, on tiptoe. "*You're* what's lovely... what's lovely is *you*."

"You like to make fun of people, Miz Carolina!"

And the Portuguese woman, sitting down also, red with heat, running her fingers through his hair, said:

"Well, that is the way things are, my darling. What I wanted to tell you was that I'm madly in love with you!"

"What?"

"I'm talking seriously. Now don't run and tell Bom-Crioulo that I'm trying to take his boyfriend away from him. Be careful, because that Negro is capable of throttling me."

"You're joking again, Miz Carolina."

"It's not a joke, my boy, not in the least," she replied, putting on a serious air. "I want you to sleep tonight, at least tonight, with this old woman of yours."

And she leaned over, limp, against Aleixo's shoulders, imitating the tenderness of a young, innocent girl.

The boy, shamefaced, tried to avoid her gaze. His mouth, shadowed by incipient adolescent down, wore a fixed smile. He shrank back into his chair and said not a word.

But the contact of his leg with the woman's leg made him feel a special warmth, a soft entanglement of his soul, a vague, delightful weariness in the very depths of his nature, a marvellous sensation of well-being.

If it were up to him, he'd have stayed in that position forever, feeling the constantly strengthening, magnetic influence of that female body on his nervous system — the nervous system of a teenager who was still a virgin.

Miz Carolina drew closer and closer to him, hugging him tight, clinging to him in a violent outburst of sexual appetite, a worn-out, used-up woman awakening to a new sensation.

"You aren't man enough to take me on," she said, draping her leg over Aleixo's knee.

And she enveloped him completely with her wide, gross Portuguese body.

"Now tell me: will you stay or won't you?"

The teenager bounded like an excited young steer, and, holding himself in the chair with both hands, trembling all over now, his face absolutely bloodless, said:

"I'll stay!"

At that, as if someone had suddenly opened the floodgates of pleasure for her, she sank her teeth into the cabin-boy's cheek, with brutal eagerness, and, grabbing him by the buttocks, eyes sparkling, face ruddy, she lifted him up and laid him down on the bed, saying:

"Over there, my little hothouse flower, over there! You're going to have a hot-blooded old Portuguese woman tonight. Forget your innocence, come on!"

She slammed the door shut and began to undress hastily, in front of Aleixo, who lay there motionless, astonished by this woman-man who was eager to deflower him right then and there, just like that, crudely, like an animal.

"Come on, you crazy little kid, get undressed too. Learn something from your old lady. Come on, because I'm hot as fire!"

Aleixo had no time to coordinate his thoughts. Miz Carolina fully absorbed him, as she seemed to transform herself before his very eyes. She, the one who was usually so gentle, so restrained, even scrupulous — she seemed to him now like some dangerous animal, exuding sensuality, like a cow in heat, overstimulated, that throws herself at the male even before he prepares his attack.

It was unbelievable!

The only thing that woman didn't do was howl!

And his astonishment increased even more when she stripped off her sweat-soaked chemise and tumbled naked into bed, panting, holding up her flabby breasts, with a strange gleam in her basilisk's eyes.

But Aleixo knew, from his experiences with Bom-Crioulo, to what extremes human animality can go, and, after the first moment of surprise, he decided that he too was made of flesh and blood, like the black man, like Miz Carolina. A night like this coming one was certainly worth it!

If only I could never, never see that nigger again, ah, I'd be so happy, the cabin-boy was thinking, as he approached a group of sailors, near the dock.

And the figure of the Portuguese landlady, very plump and smiling, her white, white teeth, her wide hips, her rosy face, danced in his imagination, like some diabolical dream.

He woke up early, before dawn. He wanted to return on board ship in the sloop that went out early to buy food at the market.

The landlady got up and made coffee for him right there in the room, without wakening anybody, as happy and exultant as a bride.

Thank God, she thought, she was well-preserved for her age; she wasn't so old as she'd imagined. She was still strong enough to wear out many a good man yet, indeed she was!

"So now you know, my baby; when Bom-Crioulo doesn't come ashore, come and give Carola a kiss. From now on I want you to call me Carola, d'you hear? It sounds nicer, between two people who like each other. Carola and 'Bitty Pretty Boy' is what we should call each other."

Dawn was breaking when the cabin-boy, still half-drunk with sleep, his eyes like slits, set out, stepping lightly, directly toward the Mineiros dock. He was very white, with great dark shadows under his eyes, and he kept repeating mechanically: "If Bom-Crioulo ever finds out!...", while his spirit kept returning to the house on Misericórdia Street, where at that very moment Miz Carolina was refreshing herself with a delicious cold shower.

VII

Bom-Crioulo was not happy on the battleship, in that redoubtable steel prison which took up all his time and whose code of discipline — a horribly heavy work-load — didn't allow him to go ashore every second day, as was customary on the other ships. Ah! he'd a thousand times rather have stayed on the corvette, a thousand times! At least there you had freedom. Separated from Aleixo now, living in the midst of a crowd of unloving strangers, he remembered sadly the good life he'd lived, together with the cabin-boy — almost a year of peace and happiness! It was certainly true, that old saw that said that all good things must come to an end.

His heart swelled with hatred of all his superior officers: a bunch of good-for-nothings! They were all the same; they all used a poor sailor as a work-horse. Who could possibly understand them? He was especially bitter against Naval Headquarters, which had ordered his transfer from the corvette to the battleship. It wouldn't have been too difficult for him to appeal to the minister, to tell some long, complicated story, and beg, on bended knee, if he had to, to be put on some other ship. And if they didn't believe him, he could go into hospital on sick leave, or he could desert and roam the world with the cabin-boy. But they didn't know him if they thought he'd do something like that. Bom-Crioulo had blood in his veins, and he was the kind of man who could live alone in a desert, if necessary. Sons of bitches!

The very first day he had the displeasure of having to stay on board. His name had been forwarded to the first mate in a special note: "Be very careful with Amaro (Bom-Crioulo). He is a model sailor when he doesn't drink, but when he has had a few, watch out! He raises a devil of a row." The officers immediately took precautionary measures.

It would be better not to let him go ashore too often. A man like that sounded almost frightening!

And it was agreed that he would have shore leave only once a month. The first day went by, and the second, and the third. The fourth was a Saturday.

"Sir, I need to go ashore," implored the black man, standing at attention, hand raised to his cap in salute.

"Not yet," muttered the first mate, paying no attention to him. "When your turn comes I'll call you."

"But sir . . ."

"I said no, now don't bother me!"

Bom-Crioulo retreated in silence, eyes cast down toward the deck, biting his lip. He was filled with a mute anger, perhaps with a desire for vengeance. Aha, so that's the way things were? he reflected later in the prow. He'd show them.

And the next morning he offered to row in the sloop that was going in to the market to buy provisions. He got in the boat, without seeming to have anything special in mind, and set out rowing with the other sailors, his cap pushed down over his forehead, very serious-looking, sitting stiffly in his place on the bench.

Sunday was dawning, splendidly, lazily, in a magnificent display of blue, cool and transparent. The mountains of the bay, Sugar Loaf, the Organ Mountains, and, far in the distance, Corcovado, without even a fleck of cloud hiding its peak, were etched in the ethereal clarity of the calm air, giving the whole scene the pleasant aspect of a watercolour painting.

A beautiful morning indeed for a boat excursion, a picnic at sea! The impassive, mysterious shape of a German steamer was making its way out of the bay. The Castle flagpole was sending signals. The warships, silent and motionless, seemed to be sleeping still.

It was almost daybreak.

"Rest on your oars!" The coxswain brought the sloop into place. They had reached the dock. The sailors, in unison, stopped their rowing and, still in unison, lowered their oars into the boat.

The market was nearby. Sloops from other ships had begun to tie up as well. Little by little it was getting light. But the square was still almost deserted. A few Portuguese boatmen wandered around among the stalls.

Bom-Crioulo got off, pretending to have to answer "a call of nature" and promising to return right away.

"It's right near here."

He slipped through the garden that adorned the square and, once he was out of sight of his companions, he dashed toward Misericórdia Street, muttering insults under his breath. The door of the house was closed. He knocked. Miz Carolina was snoring. He knocked again, impatiently, banging on the door

90

with his fists.

The counter clerk in the bakery across the way came out to see who was knocking so persistently.

Who could it be? A black man!

Finally someone came to open the door: a fat gentleman with a long beard, wearing suspenders, and with a face like a jailbird, stood back to let the sailor in.

"Good morning!"

"Good morning!" answered the bearded man.

"Who is it?" asked the muffled voice of the landlady from upstairs.

"It's me, Miz Carolina; please excuse all the noise."

"Oh, it's you, Bom-Crioulo? What a commotion! Here so early? We don't see you around any more! the key's on the nail there."

"Thank you."

And soon Bom-Crioulo was throwing open the window of his room, taking the morning cool full on his face. He'd like to see if they could drag him out of there now. Like hell they could! He was in his own house, well hidden away. He was no work-horse!

And he thought of the cabin-boy. Did Aleixo still remember him? Because in this world people are always fooling themselves. The more you like a person, the more that person treats you like dirt. And Bom-Crioulo was no fool, he wasn't.

He opened the drawers of the table, he checked the furniture, he moved papers about, like someone looking for something, he examined the bed, sniffing, feeling. The bottle of hair-oil wasn't in the corner cupboard and had been cleaned out. The bottle of Florida cologne, which he'd left almost full, was two-thirds empty now. The tin of shoe-polish was lying upside-down on the floor, at the foot of the iron washstand; the floor itself was a mess of cigarette butts and spittle.

"I can guess!" murmured Bom-Crioulo, giving his own interpretation to that customary disorder. "I can guess!"

At that precise moment the carillon of the São José church[1] began to ring out the melody of *Les cloches de Corneville*, filling the air with its festive, lively sound, multiplying it, in notes of Offenbachian clarity, as if some marvellous crystal instrument were suspended in the air. Instinctively the sailor

---

[1] St. Joseph's church, on the street of the same name, is still there and its carillon (1883) still plays arias from *Les cloches de Corneville*, an operetta by Planquette (1877), on a silly libretto by Clairville and Gabet.

began to hum the familiar old strains of the operetta:

Ding, ding, ding,
Ding, ding, dong!

Deep down inside he was happy today, he felt in a good mood, with all the impulsiveness of a mischievous child, like a bird set free. It even surprised him! He'd not wakened up in the morning feeling so good for a long time now.

The portrait of the emperor smiled benevolently down on him, with his thick beard, like an indulgent patriarch. The emperor was *his* man. Those so-called "republicans" spoke badly of him because the old man had feelings and loved the people.

He lit a cigarette and stretched out on the bed.

Ah, this was the life! They could talk all they liked about battleships: he'd rather have his bed, his comfort, his rest.

A ray of sunlight was coming in through the window now, and the bells continued their interminable musical refrain.

Ding, ding, ding,
Ding, ding, dong!

"Bom-Crioulo, Bom-Crioulo!"

"Oooh! What is it?"

"Wake up, my boy, it's almost noon."

"Noon?"

"Yes, can't you see how high the sun is in the sky?"

Miz Carolina, seeing that Bom-Crioulo had not come down yet, went up to wake him up. Amaro was in a deep sleep, stretched out on the bed, with his mouth open, his cap down over his eyes, a thread of spittle running down his chin, absolutely motionless. His arms hung as loose as a corpse's. On entering the room, the landlady started and turned white. Dear God! Could he be dead? But the black man snored loudly. What a fright! She approached timidly, so as not to startle him, and when he opened his eyes he saw her, there in front of him, plump and smiling, all dressed in new clothes, wearing a white apron.

"Wake up, lazybones!" she said, slapping the black man's thigh. "Come on, get up. This isn't the time of day to sleep."

"Bom-Crioulo slowly raised himself, wiping his chin with his sleeve, and asked what time it was. His body felt weak, his eyes were red, he had a peculiar taste in his mouth.

"So what happened today?" asked the landlady.

"I ran away," said the sailor, with complete naturalness, stretching his arms in a yawn. "I came on the market sloop, and I'm here without permission."

"That's crazy, my boy! They could have you arrested."

"Sons of bitches! I'm nobody's slave. I'll run away as often as I feel like it, and nobody can stop me."

"Keep your head, my boy. You have to do things the proper way."

"To hell with the proper way, ma'am! Since I've been on that ship I haven't had any rest. It's too much!"

"Now, now, son, be patient. God will help you."

"It's the old story: trust in the Virgin and don't run away."

"Well, it's your affair, and theirs," said the woman, putting an end to the discussion, staring at the portrait of the emperor as if she had never seen it before.

"Just one question," said Bom-Crioulo. "Has Aleixo been ashore?"

"He came on Thursday, if I'm not mistaken."

And the black man counted on his fingers:

"Thursday, Friday, Saturday, Sunday: yesterday would have been his day to come."

"These days the two of you never seem to meet. You don't get together any more. Let's see," she continued. "Would you like to eat something, or have you already had breakfast?"

"No, nothing. I'll have something to eat in the restaurant."

"I can send out and buy something."

"No, thanks. I need to take a walk, to stretch my legs and get a little exercise."

"Be careful. Watch out for the officers."

And going toward the staircase, she added:

"Well, I just came to wake you up. Goodbye."

"Goodbye, ma'am. So the kid has come ashore only once, eh?"

"Just once, poor little fellow."

And the black man continued thinking about the cabin-boy. He sat at the table, depressed, picking his nails mechanically with a match. "Things" weren't going well at all. He had to make a decision: to leave Aleixo, to break off with him once and for all, and live on board, or maybe to find some girl of his own colour and live peacefully with her. He was getting too thin, he wasn't eating, he had no rest, he was in a state in which he could easily fall sick, catch some disease — and it was all because of "Mr. Aleixo". If he could see him every day, at least, as he did on the corvette...But like this, far from each other? It wasn't worth it; it was letting yourself be played for a fool.

And, picking up his cap, with an expression of distaste, he said to himself:

"Well, that's enough! It has to be settled, today or tomorrow."

He slammed the door shut, locked it and went out on the street, his hands in his pockets, feeling quite hopeless.

Miz Carolina was inside, spreading out clothes to dry in the yard, and she stayed there.

The stones in the street glittered under the noonday sun, directly overhead. In the bar on the nearest corner, there was a crowd of people, and every passer-by became one more spectator, one more gaping face. The people who lived on the street were leaning out their windows, craning their necks, with a questioning look in their eyes. An official from the fire department went running by toward the place where the "incident" was occurring. People in passing trolleys stood up and looked. The baker, in his shirt-sleeves, with a pencil stuck behind his ear, came to the door of the bakery, shuffling in his slippers.

Bom-Crioulo at first thought it was a fight and rushed in, trying to push through the crowd. But it was a man suffering an attack of epilepsy,[1] who was rolling about on the ground, frothing at the mouth, his face bathed in blood, his beard dirty with sand, twisting in horrible contortions.

He had fallen down suddenly as he left the bar.

"He'd drunk a lot of rum." the bar-owner said, remorsefully. "If I'd known, I'd not have sold him any."

Two policeman tried to lift the man to his feet, but they desisted.

"No use, the brute's as heavy as lead!"

"Wait a minute, wait a minute!" Bom-Crioulo leapt into action. "You people are no good for anything at all."

The crowd drew back, amazed, and watched Bom-Crioulo lift the man up with his two hands and carry him on his shoulders to Misericórdia Hospital,[2] without visible effort, as if he were carrying a child.

It hurt him to see that poor man lying there like that, in the middle of the street, surrounded by on-lookers, twisting around like an ownerless animal. A scene like that oppressed his heart, frightened him, upset him. Maybe he was the father of a family, poor fellow, or some unfortunate wretch. The falling sickness was a horrible disease! Already, on another occasion, he had saved a drunken woman from being run over by a trolley-car.

---

[1] The original has *gota* (gout), which was a Brazilian popular name for epilepsy.

[2] Misericórdia Hospital, for which the street in this novel is named, is the "mercy" or "charity" hospital of Rio de Janeiro. It is located at the upper end of Misericórdia Street.

And the Portuguese bar-owner, the baker, the policemen, a doctor who happened to be passing by, the owner of the butcher-shop, everybody praised the black man's strength.

"Yes, sirree, he's strong enough to kill an ox! Seamen are real men!"

"Two policemen couldn't lift the man, but the nigger did it all by himself!"

"The navy's still the navy."

A soldier who was present raised his voice in protest:

"No, sir, it's not like that at all. He's not the only hero around. There're strong men in the army, too, just as there are weaklings in the navy, too, real featherweights."

No one said anything more, and little by little the crowd thinned out, until only two or three people were left there chatting.

Bom-Crioulo came back from the hospital almost immediately, with his long stride, swinging his arms, his cap pulled down, as usual, beaming. Really the man did weigh a lot, but it was a disgrace that two policemen couldn't lift him. There were *two* of them, remember!

And, addressing the bar-owner, he said:

"A triple white rum, please."

The Portuguese bar-owner, very well-mannered, without taking his eyes off the sailor, filled the measure. "Yes," he murmured smilingly, "it *is* a disgrace for Brazil. Now, in Portugal..."

Bom-Crioulo coughed, spat, drained the glass and uttered an exclamation of repugnance: "Ugh! Whoo! What the devil! That's like drinking fire!"

He undid the tip of his kerchief, where he usually carried his change — a poor, dirty kerchief, with a pattern around the edges.

"These are my last *vinténs*,"[1] he said, "what's left of my wages, my miserable wages. Luckily I don't need to worry as long as a Portuguese lady called Carolina is still alive."

The bar-owner winked at him: "Aha, aha! You're a sharp one, aren't you?"

"What can you do, my friend? A man has to live.".

He had a very light head, a very weak head for alcohol. A shot of white rum, an insignificant amount of spirits, a half-pint of wine would turn his eyes red as coals, would make him lose his balance, would go right to his head. And when he drank too

---

[1]Plural of *vintém*, a former Brazilian coin, worth twenty *reis*.

much, at some party or celebration, now and then — Lord save us! Nobody could handle him then. His strength would be doubled; he wouldn't recognize his friends; he would insult the whole human race; he would threaten everyone, shaking his fists, pushing his cap down over his eyes, staggering around — it was terrifying, terrible!

That day it seemed as though Bom-Crioulo had decided to get drunk on purpose. Shortly after downing the white rum, half-dazed already, walking very erect and tall so as not to show any sign of weakness, but with his vision already blurred and a sour taste in his mouth, he left the corner bar without any fixed destination and set out toward the Pharoux dock. He walked along sadly, glassy-eyed, seeing double images of houses wheeling around his head, leaning against walls, muttering incomprehensible phrases to himself, completely changed already.

His ideas were all mixed up, in a state of murky agitation like that of someone's who's on the point of losing his mind. Everything darkened before his eyes, and he felt like doing something crazy, like sitting down in the middle of the street, and opening his mouth and talking nonsense, like a madman.

"I'm getting out of here, but I'm going straight back on board," he muttered. "I'll show that scum! I'm going because I want to go, because I'm a free man!"

And he thumped on his chest.

"Sons of bitches! I saved that man with the falling sickness, I did an act of charity, now let them talk! Parrots can talk but they can't see in the dark, as that captain used to say, I can't remember his name . . ."

It was two o'clock in the afternoon. The shops had closed down: the lumber warehouses, all the business establishments, with the exception of a very few cafés, were shuttered at that Sunday-afternoon hour.

A few passers-by strolled along slowly, taking the sun, silent, thinking about life, with the sluggish tread of cattle coming home at evening.

Bom-Crioulo went down the street, reeling in zigzag fashion, paying no attention to anyone. But when he reached the Palace Square, a stray dog began to bark at him, jumping at him, following him, running in circles around him. Other dogs joined the first one, and soon an infernal uproar surrounded the black man, increasing little by little, irritating, deafening. Young boys spurred the dogs on with shouts and whistles. The Portuguese on the dock[1] were alarmed. Who was it? Who could it be? The big nigger, the sailor!

Meanwhile, Bom-Crioulo kept on walking, staggering, recovering his balance, shooing the dogs away, threatening them with stones, howling insults: "Sons of bitches!"

Everybody watched him turn toward the dock.

"Hey, sloop!" he shouted, seeing a warboat floating, motionless, with a crew of rowers, some distance off shore.

There was no answer.

The sea was calm. The water glistened like burnished steel. The air was suffocating!

On the other side of the bay, far in the distance, in Niterói, the tiny white tower of a church was visible, long and thin as an obelisk.

Boats for hire floated silently, shaded by awnings, tied to one another, at their landing-place, between the two ferry terminals,[2] quiet and lethargic.

"Oh, sloop!" roared the black man.

The boat didn't move. It was as if there were no one aboard. The sailors pretended not to hear.

"You bunch of donkeys! Come alongside with that piece of filth you're rowing!"

And he opened his mouth in a tremendous volley of insults, clenching his fists threateningly, deploying all the obscene, dirty vocabulary of the barracks against his fellow-sailors, shouting at the top of his lungs that he was a free man, that he had to do it, that it had to happen!

"Scum! I don't need you for anything! For anything at all!"

But when he turned around, he bumped into a Portuguese boatman, who was standing there by his side, holding an oar, laughing silently.

"And you too, 'Galician'! You're laughing, because you haven't got it in the puss yet!" said Bom-Crioulo, giving the man a shove.

---

[1] These Portuguese are the boatmen, owners and/or oarsmen of boats for hire, with whom Bom-Crioulo is constantly having fights. (See Chapter 1, p. 34, and Chapter 2, p. 41.)

[2] The two ferry-terminals are that of the ferry-boats which connect Rio and Niterói (see page 67) and that of the ferries going to other points in Guanabara Bay, such as Paquetá Island. The boatmen's landing-place seems to have been located between the two, in a narrow slip.

The Portuguese frowned and looked the black man over from head to toe, without saying a word.

"And you don't need to stare at me like that, either! If you don't believe me I'll make you drink salt water."

"Go away, my good fellow," murmured the Portuguese good-naturedly. "Go away."

"What?"

"You're in bad shape."

"What did you say, 'Galician', what did you say?"

And he confronted the Portuguese, unbuttoning his shirt and puffing up his chest, taking off his cap.

"Please don't get me angry, sir."

"I'll smash your face in right here, 'Galician'."

The Portuguese lost control of himself. A flash of rage gleamed in his eyes, his face turned red, his oar dropped from his hand, and he charged Bom-Crioulo, trying to knock him down right then and there, in body-to-body combat. He was short, strong, and freckled, with a tawny moustache and a very ruddy complexion.

The fight began immediately. The dock, the whole space between the two ferry stations, filled up with noisy, excited spectators, who came running like attack troops from all corners of the square. "Fight! Fight!"

And, in their desperate struggle, the two men little by little shifted toward the square, moving away from the untenable terrain where they couldn't manoeuvre freely for fear of falling into the water. They were locked together, body to body, tangled round each other, and it was an open question as to which was stronger — they were equal in muscular force.

The war sloop had come closer.

There was great excitement among the small boats: the alarm had been spread on the dock and in all the neighbourhood.

"Separate! Separate!" shouted the boatmen.

Whistles and hisses, barking dogs, shouts of "You aren't man enough! You aren't man enough!" all mingled in an extraordinary tumult that echoed all over the square.

Suddenly, with a fearful wrench, Bom-Crioulo broke free of his opponent's hold and quickly, lightly, stealthily pulled something out of his waistband. All the spectators saw, horrified, the steel of a knife glittering in the sailor's hand now.

"Now it's coming!" said a voice from the crowd.

And the crowd drew back, scattered, left the field free to the combatants. But the outcry grew louder and louder: "Strike! Strike! You aren't man enough to!"

The Portuguese, with his clothes in tatters and his hair ruffled up, ran away as fast as he could, but the black man, seeing policemen approaching, shouted threateningly, brandishing his weapon furiously:

"If any of you think you're a man, come take me!"

The figure of the "Galician" had disappeared: his anger was directed now against the crowd and the police. Nobody dared approach the wild man; just the look in his eyes was enough to frighten you.

Four o'clock on the ferry-terminal clock.

Shortly thereafter a naval officer landed at the dock. Bom-Crioulo was waiting for him, fearless: "Don't come any closer or you'll get it!"

He was a first lieutenant, and he was accompanied by sailors.

"Take that man in," he ordered, stopping some distance away.

"Don't come any closer! Don't come any closer!" shouted the black man, staggering, knife raised in the air.

The men split up, three to each side, and marched forward fearlessly, swords drawn.

It was a moment of wonder and bated breath.

The huge body of the Negro, redoubling its movements of acrobatic clownishness, twisted and turned, avoiding the bayonets, as though he were being moved by some hidden wire-spring mechanism. "Don't come any closer! Don't come any closer!"

But when, with astonishing force, he leapt to the right, a stronger arm than his pinned him down on the left, and Bom-Crioulo, the invincible Bom-Crioulo, found himself caught, trapped like a wild animal!

The victorious throng now flocked to the scene of the conflict, with no fear of being attacked, commenting on the fight, and a crowd of on-lookers accompanied the sailor to the water's edge.

What a struggle it was to get him on the sloop! The black man fought and bit, in a paroxysm of rabid desperation, insulting them, calling down curses on them.

Finally they got him on board by sheer force, and the clean, white sloop cut smoothly though the quiet bay.

VIII

The captain of the battleship, a fine figure of an aristocratic military gentleman, impeccable and temperamental, was the same officer, the very same one concerning whom, in Bom-Crioulo's rough euphemism, "stories were told."

A vague, obscure legend had grown up around his name, turning him into a kind of Gilles de Rais, though less fearful than his historical counterpart — a man completely indifferent to the fair sex, who sought out instead his innate, ideal model of beauty in male adolescents, among people of his own social class.

Lies, perhaps, vulgar insinuations.

When they had nothing to do, on calm, moonlit nights, the sailors told tales among themselves, legends and rumours often made up on the spot, in the heat of conversation.

The captain, they said, wasn't a skirt-chaser at all; he was a strange character, uninterested in women, who preferred to live in his own way, with his own people, with his sailors.

And there was always a touch of respectful hypocrisy, of malicious hesitation when the captain was mentioned.

Be that as it may, no one spoke disrespectfully of him. Everyone wanted him to remain as he was, enigmatic, a mystery, with his distinguished, aristocratic bearing, gentle at times, an implacable disciplinarian, a model officer.

Bom-Crioulo, however, had never really liked him; he regarded him with a certain distrust and could not get used to that honeyed voice, to that languid protectorial air which the captain so cleverly assumed when he was in a good mood. He avoided him as one would avoid a sworn enemy. Why? Bom-Crioulo himself didn't know. An instinctive repugnance, a natural antipathy — opposing forces that repelled each other.

That man was born to do me wrong, thought the black man, superstitiously.

Immediately after the fight he had been shackled and fettered. The image of the captain shone through the haze of his drunkeness and pursued him remorselessly all night, not leaving him in peace for one second — an image that at one moment

100

was terrible, threatening and unpardoning, and the next moment, tender, gentle and tolerant.

So he slept that night in an iron tomb, a sort of narrow, lightless cage with room for only one person. Shut in there, unable to move, because his feet and hands were fettered, he fell asleep finally when the rest of the ship was waking up, at the first notes of reveille, just before dawn. In his sleep he saw the figure of the Portuguese boatman bending over him with a knife, taunting him: "Come on, nigger, come on, I'll show you!" He was a husky man and his clothes were spattered with blood; his beard was long and his eyes flashed.

They were going to come to blows, but Aleixo wouldn't let them; he said that the police would come and arrest them, that it wasn't worth fighting over nothing at all. So, because he liked the boy so much, Bom-Crioulo ran away, leaving the boatman there in the middle of a wide square, full of trees.

He was soon awakened to reality, however. It was eleven o'clock. The door of the dungeon had been opened and, without even having eaten anything, he was going to be punished. They were waiting for the captain to arrive to begin the ceremony. Light filled the solitary-confinement cell and illuminated the prisoner's face.

"Get up," ordered the sergeant on guard.

Bom-Crioulo couldn't even move: they had to hold him up. An iron gag was pressed against his mouth. His gaze was filled with a sad, dumb indignation.

He got up, stumbling and swaying, his eyes like two burning torches, his cheeks bruised, almost purple, because he had fallen asleep with his head on his knee, in the posture of an Indian mummy. But the fresh air of the morning revived him; the light that flooded the atmosphere cheered him up; he felt his whole being vibrate; and he offered himself up to the punishment that awaited him without fear, undaunted and calm, even as he nourished a very personal hatred, in the depths of his human nature, for those people who surrounded him, delighting, no doubt, in his misfortune. He had nobody on his side — he was a derelict, a poor lost soul. Even Aleixo, where was Aleixo now?

And the memory disturbed him. Yes, Aleixo was the cause of it all. All the time he had lived together with the cabin-boy, he had never really got drunk; every now and then he'd drink a shot of white rum, to warm his innards, and that was enough. Now he needed a triple shot, and he liked another one after that. Ah, Mr. Aleixo, Mr. Aleixo!...

Just as in the previous case, on the corvette, there was a "general muster", with the whole crew standing in military formation, in the stern, on the quarterdeck.

It was a terrible punishment.

"I don't want the crew of this ship to forget these words," harangued the captain. "Disobedience, drunkenness and pederasty are very serious crimes. Don't forget!"

And, as before, Bom-Crioulo remained completely silent under the caning. He took it all without a word or a cry, writhing at every blow, in the awful pain that racked him from head to toe, as if his whole body were one great, open, living, bloody wound. An imperceptible rattling groan, short and dry, expressing all his anguish, died away in his throat without emerging. His facial muscles dilated in twitching contractions; his blood roared convulsively inside him, in his arteries, in his heart, in the innermost recesses of his body, throbbing, rushing, in an extraordinary flood!

He bore it all with the savage pride of a wounded animal, which cannot take revenge because it's been made a prisoner, and which dies without a whimper, its eyes ablaze with impotent anger!

The burning light of noon fell with a vague, universal sadness over everything. From beyond the harbour bar a faint, cool breeze blew, heavy with the smell of mud flats and seaweed, ruffling the water. The city, across the way, ranged like an amphitheatre, glowed among its mountains in the languid apathy of that sultry hour. The shape of the battleship, elongated and motionless in the middle of the bay, with its huge battering-ram, with its canvas sunshade, stood out in splendour, far from the other ships, far from land, like a fantasy, an architectural masterpiece!

As the last blow was being delivered, Bom-Crioulo staggered and fell flat on the deck, bathed in blood. There was not one strip of skin on his back that the whip had not touched. He fell, as he had to fall, when his body had been completely drained of strength, when the punishment had reached an in-human level and pain had conquered will-power.

Only then did the ship's doctor appear, trembling and nervous, saying "it's nothing, it's nothing; bring the bottle of ether, and water, a little water."

The captain came up also, but retreated immediately with his disdainful air of aristocratic snobbery, saying "Don't forget! Don't forget!"

And in a few moments a sloop without a pennant set out,

bearing the sailor to the hospital.

"Get away, devil ship, get away!" exclaimed Bom-Crioulo, turning toward the battleship at one point during the trip. "Get away!"

Aleixo was free that day, and he went ashore quite early, about one o'clock, driven by a deep longing which had by now made him a slave to the landlady. He was afraid of meeting Bom-Crioulo, of having to put up with his whims, his nigger smell, his bullish instincts, and remembering all these things made him feel sad and displeased with himself. He had ended up despising the black man, almost hating him, full of aversion, full of disgust for that animal in the form of a man, who said he was his friend only in order to enjoy him sexually. He felt sorry for Bom-Crioulo, he pitied him, for, after all, he owed him many favours, but he didn't like him: no, he had never liked him!

He went up the stairs slowly, step by step, carefully holding on to the wall, his ears pricked, holding his breath. Luckily, the upstairs door was open.

Now and then he stepped too heavily, and his calfskin boots squeaked dully. There'd be hell to pay if Bom-Crioulo was there.

He advanced, still cautiously, to the dining-room. No one there! He proceeded into the kitchen, and, from the window that looked onto the yard, he saw the landlady there, bending over a pile of wet clothing, in her wooden clogs, her skirt tucked up and wearing no coat, busy at her work, singing away. An instinct made her turn around and look up; her first reaction was a cry of surprise and delight: "Ah, my little one, my little one! I'm coming right away. Wait for me, eh?"

Aleixo put his finger to his lips in a plea for silence and, pointing up to the attic, asked, leaning out the window, if Bom-Crioulo was there.

"What Bom-Crioulo?" said Miz Carolina in a loud voice, extravagantly, taking no precautions. "There isn't any Bom-Crioulo here! Your old gal is here all by herself, my baby. Just let me rinse out these things I have here, won't you? I'll be right up."

But the cabin-boy couldn't wait: he went down to the yard to look more closely at that full, rich female body in washer-woman's clothing; his eyes contemplated her ecstatically.

Really, the landlady was irresistible to a teenager like Aleixo, inexperienced as he was in this kind of adventure, with his male sexuality just beginning to develop.

Miz Carolina was wearing a blouse and a short skirt that came down only to her knees; on her head she wore a large calico bandanna tied around her neck.

"Don't come any closer, my baby," she said, realising Aleixo's intentions. "Look, just let me finish this, please?"

The cabin-boy acted offended: "Oh, by all means finish, by all means." And then, coming up closer, he added:

"I only came down because I wanted to see you up close."

"You're making fun of me, eh? You're making fun of your old lady."

"Making fun, nothing. It's the truth."

The landlady burst into peals of clear, joyful laughter, deep and vibrant, her hips shaking, her head wagging hysterically:

"That's my rosebud! That's my little bitty pretty rosebud!" And she laughed and laughed like someone possessed. Aleixo grew annoyed:

"All right, I'm going."

"Oh, no, don't. It's only a joke! If you leave, I'll be angry. Yes, I will! yes, I will!"

And she put on an air of tenderness, softening her voice:

"Stay, my bitty pretty boy, stay here with your old gal."

He smiled faintly, and they started to chat again, like good friends.

They stayed there, under the zinc roof, for a long, long time, the cabin-boy sitting on the edge of the cistern, cross-legged, and the landlady hurrying to finish her washing.

Outside that little space cooled by the water, the sun shone with a blazing, searing strength. The dry grass in the yard was as hot as fire to the touch, stunted, desolate and autumnal-looking. Somewhere nearby, a pet parrot shrieked stridently. It was very quiet. The water sang ceaselessly as it fell from the spout into the cistern, running, running.

Aleixo hung up his blue-flannel sailor-shirt and sat in his knit undershit, listening to the song of the water, while Miz Carolina rinsed her clothes.

They talked about Bom-Crioulo and laughed hypocritically at the black man, in low voices.

"A good fellow," pontificated the landlady, with just a touch of irony in her voice.

"Good to make a bonfire of!" added Aleixo.

They knew nothing about the fight. The landlady simply told him that Bom-Crioulo had gone out the day before, just after noon, and he hadn't come back. Of course they must have taken him prisoner.

A clock struck the hour.

"What time is it?" she asked.

"Four o'clock," said the boy.

"Heavens, I'm going to stop, I'm stopping. I'll leave the rest for tomorrow."

"That's right! That's enough work. The clothes aren't going to run away," said Aleixo, getting up.

And his eyes, bright with desire, eager for pleasure, alit treacherously on Miz Carolina's bare neck and shoulders.

And, as if she felt the sting of that gaze in her own body, as if she felt its living heat, its magnetic force, its physical, material, irresistible power, she went up to the cabin-boy and murmured in his ear, producing in him the vague, undefinable effect of a nervous shock: "Let's take a bath."

"Here?"

"Why not?"

"Somebody might see."

"We'll close the door to the street. I don't have any tenants right now."

Aleixo didn't accept or refuse. He yawned and stretched his entire body, twisting it in a partial spasm, feeling a wonderful chill, a thrill, a marvellous turbulence ripple through his nervous system, going down the small of the back and spreading through his whole organism.

The landlady quickly went upstairs, to her apartment, and came back beaming, almost at once.

She insisted on undressing the boy herself, taking off his knit shirt, taking off his trousers, stripping him in her sight. Bom-Crioulo had already told her that Aleixo had a "woman's body".

Then she began to undress too.

The cistern was so full it was practically overflowing. You could see the bottom through the clear, cool water.

No one saw them in that primitive nakedness, face to face — the soft, ample body of the Portuguese woman contrasting with the lean, muscular, ideal beauty of the adolescent — scandalously nude, sinfully Biblical, in the silence of a little yard, hidden away from the sun which scattered its tawny golden light around the small porch that shielded them!

What they did, both before and after their bath, no one will ever know. The walls of the yard enveloped and concealed all that mysterious erotic scene enacted there on Misericórdia Street on a splendid November day.

Miz Carolina had finally had her wish fulfilled, the wish of a worn-out woman — to have a boyish, beardless youth as her lover, innocent enough to be still capable of blushing, almost the ideal lover, who would be to her what a pet is to its owner — loyal, sincere, devoted to the point of self-sacrifice.

Aleixo rejuvenated her like some strange, miraculous aphrodisiac or elixir. She felt like a different person since she had taken up with the boy: her nerves were stronger, her appetite was better, her soul was filled with the extraordinary happiness of a bride on her honeymoon, her whole being celebrated in a festive exuberance of new life, in a torrential outburst of joy — her body felt light, her spirit was calm. Aleixo belonged to her at last; he was wholly hers. She had him trapped now like a beautiful bird which has let itself be caged; she had taught him the secrets of love, and he had enjoyed it all enormously and sworn never to leave her, never again.

The cabin-boy, in turn, felt what any teenager would feel — a fatal attraction toward the landlady, an overwhelming desire to have her all the time, all the time, at any hour of the day, an irresistible desire to bite her, smell her, feel her in a frenzy of pleasure — the powerful, wild instincts of an insatiable young steer.

The afternoon went by quickly. After supper (soup, boiled beef and São Tomé bananas as well as wine supplied by the butcher), they went into the front room. Aleixo wanted to look at her photograph album; the landlady brought it out. And, sitting together on the old sofa, almost embracing each other, the boy very curious, wanting to know who was who in the photographs, the woman bending over, her still damp hair unbound and flowing loose, explaining each figure in detail, scenes from Europe, memories of Portugal and the islands — they awaited nightfall.

It grew darker. Miz Carolina went to light the gas, complaining of the heat: "I'd like to never come out of the water, to live in it, to die in the water, floating."

Aleixo laughed amusedly, thinking perhaps of the resemblance between the Portuguese woman and a large, round-bellied corvette.

"Now, just tell me one thing, my baby. Do you really love me or is this all a whim of yours, a game?"

And she smiled as she sat down:

"But listen, tell me the truth! Watch out if you go telling me lies."

Then he told her that he loved her from the bottom of his heart, and he swore again that he'd die beside her in the same bed — next to her, side by side.

"And if you die on board ship, at sea?"

"Don't talk like that," murmured the boy, in a sad voice. She immediately regretted her words and showered him with kisses.

"No, you won't die at sea. It was a joke, it was a joke."

The cabin-boy's smooth beardless face wore a transient expression of virginal tenderness, of everything that was fleeting and delicate, the melancholy whiteness of certain flowers, the pure, honest modesty of a schoolgirl — and it was precisely that, that undefinable *something*, that innocent poetry breathing from Aleixo's features, that moved the Portuguese woman, touching the sensitive cords of her derelict, worn-out old heart. It was really a pity, she thought, to see that feminine face, that woman's body, that little marble statue, given over to the rough paws of a sailor, a black man. Probably the lad had been seduced, had been forced into the rôle. She was actually doing him good; it was an act of charity. What he was doing with the Negro was a villainy, after all, it was an abomination, a sin, a crime! If Aleixo was going to be ruined at the hands of a black man, it was better that a woman, like her, should try to save him. Both of them would profit from it, both he and she.

But Aleixo couldn't forget Bom-Crioulo. The figure of the black man followed him everywhere, aboard and ashore, whether he wanted it to or not, with the insistence of remorse. He really sincerely wanted to hate Bom-Crioulo, to forget him forever, to blot him out of his mind like an evil thought, like some strange, feverish obsession. But he couldn't; it was all in vain! The reproving, rebuking aspect of the sailor was indelibly imprinted on his mind: he constantly remembered Bom-Crioulo's hard, rippling muscles, his vengeful, unforgiving nature, his extraordinary temperament — a strange hybrid of viciousness and tolerance — his fits of passion, his criminal tendencies, and all this, all these memories, frightened him, made his blood run cold with fear, with a vague shiver of panic, something latent, something painful. His ecstasies with the Portuguese landlady were incomplete; his lips trembled with the smile of someone bearing false-witness, every time she praised him in order to heap abuse on the black man.

All that night was a frenzy of pleasure and sensuality. Miz Carolina gave full vent to her pronounced hermaphroditic tendencies,[1] with kisses, embraces and violent suctions.

---

[1] Original has "hermafrodismo agudo." In modern parlance this would be "lesbian tendencies" or "bisexuality."

IX

It was a sad life that Bom-Crioulo was leading now, in the
naval hospital, far from Misericórdia Street and from the only
object of his affection, subjected to a monastic time-table and
way of life, eating scantily, listening at all hours to the groans of
other patients, which entered his soul like a chant of foreboding,
like the painful expression of his own abandonment, shut up
within the four walls of a dismal hospital-room — he, who loved
freedom with savage enthusiasm, and whose fondest wish was
to live forever in the company of Aleixo, ungrateful Aleixo.

The image of the boy, sleek and curvaceous, flitted tempting-
ly through his imagination, seducing him, transporting him to a
world of delights, to an atmosphere of sensuality and lust, the
mysterious silence of a life devoted to a secret love, the supreme
pleasures of the flesh, all the ecstasies of a passion now
bordering on madness.

Absence only increased his despair, and that melancholy
invalid existence bored him intensely. It was an indescribable
punishment for someone like him who craved freedom and love
— absolute freedom to do as his nature bade him do and physical
love for a being of his own sex, an infinitely beloved being like
Aleixo. He had never heard anything more about Aleixo, he had
never seen him again, they had never again exchanged even a
simple glance.

Meanwhile, what a crowd of memories peopled his brain at
night, when he alone, Bom-Crioulo, eyes wide open in the
darkness, staring at the ceiling of the sick-room, kept watch, he
alone, awake, in all that place! What a world of memories, dear
God! He saw, as if he were really looking at them, the body of
the cabin boy, his blue gaze and pale features, the cool little
room on Misericórdia Street, stuck up there like a garret, right
under the eaves, the canvas bed, the picture of the emperor on
the wall, very solemn, with an air of infinite goodwill; he saw
everything that had surrounded him in the voluptuous nest
where he had lived so many days of happiness. He lay thinking
for hours and hours, floating in a slow-moving rapture, in a

tranquil ecstasy, reliving, chapter by chapter, the story of his love. And from that ecstasy, he would fall into a deep, inexplicable depression, a special state compounded of jealousy and sick tenderness. He imagined things, like a man who has lost his powers of reason. Did Aleixo still care for him? Of course not. If he still cared for him, he would have sought him out wherever he was; but Aleixo had never bothered to do so, never again, since the day of their separation. Who knows? A new love affair.

The black man's heart filled with hatred, while at the same time he felt it swell with desire to have the boy forever.

He wanted him, yes, he did, but he wanted him pure of any bodily contact but his own; he wanted him as before, for himself alone, living side by side with him, obedient to his whims, faithful to the rules of a shared, quiet existence, full of mutual devotion.

He couldn't put the cabin-boy out of his mind, and it was now that that love of his, that sick obsession, redoubled its prodigious strength and drove him toward the boy, awakening a jealousy that had seemed dormant, touching sensibilities that had lost their former keenness. The Bom-Crioulo of the days of the corvette, the sensual boy-lover, full of inexpressible longings, chasing the novice sailor like some male catching scent of a girl who has just recently fallen into a life of vice, the erotomanic Bom-Crioulo of Misericórdia Street, bowing in ecstasy before a nude adolescent, like some savage from Zanzibar before the sacred idol of an African cult — that Bom-Crioulo miraculously reappeared.

There he lay in hospital, neglected and alone, groaning over his inconsolable sorrows, dragging around the rags and tatters of his soul, howling, like a poor ownerless dog, howling curses against the evil fate that had separated him from Aleixo, curses against God, against everything!

The sick-room windows opened out on the sea, opposite the Organ Mountains; they looked out on the melancholy back of the bay. In the ward, ten iron beds were ranged symmetrically in line, their red wool blankets folded half-over; the bright blood color contrasted with the whiteness of the sheets. As in all the wards, the faint smell of disinfectants permeated everything, that vague odour characteristic of hospitals and morgues, which becomes sometimes almost unbearable, like a whiff from an open tomb. The patients, in their white cotton uniforms, could walk around and were allowed to go outside for recreation on the hospital grounds, if they had special permission from the doctor in charge of their case. Each ward had its own specialist.

Bom-Crioulo had been placed with the patients suffering from scrofula, in the large ward looking out over the sea, from which some of the most beautiful features of the Brazilian landscape could be seen and enjoyed. But Bom-Crioulo was indifferent to everything but the cabin-boy. The memory of Aleixo tormented him terribly; no one had seen him smile since he'd entered the hospital.

Sullen, his eyes hostile and threatening, avoiding the company of the other patients, he couldn't forget, he couldn't put out of his mind one nightmarish idea — the cabin-boy in the arms of another man. Ah! That was enough to deprive him of his peace of mind, to turn him into a miserable victim, tossing and twisting in the pangs of a brutal attack of jealousy. Aleixo made him suffer whole nights and days, like a bird fluttering around in a tiny iron cage. Yes, he really loved him, he loved the boy madly; he would rather have him than all the beautiful women in the world!

While his wounds were healing, those purple tattoo marks which the caning had left on his body, a great emptiness seemed to open up in his rough sailor's soul; a terrible sense of despair gripped him whenever he thought of the cabin-boy, of the cruel boy who had taught him to love and who was making him undergo the sufferings of the damned. Bom-Crioulo felt completely changed: something deep and serious, which he himself couldn't explain, something like the presentiment of some fatal misfortune, turned him morose, drew him away from the pleasures of human company and gave him an odd air of concealed malice.

"This isn't a hospital, this is hell!" he would mumble to himself, pursing his lips in grimaces of savage rage. His patience was reaching its limits.

He'd already asked once to be discharged, but they took it as just a caprice of his, so why bother asking? He might die, but he wasn't going to act like a weakling. He was a man, what the hell! And a man has to show the world why he was born a man.

He ended up flying into rages at everybody. The male nurses were idiots! The cooks belonged in a third-class eating-house! He even insulted the doctor, as soon as the latter had turned his back on him.

His only consolation in this galley-slave's neglect, in this kind of spiritual widowhood, was a picture of Aleixo, a cheap photograph taken on Hospício Street, when he and the boy still lived together on the corvette. It showed the cabin-boy in his blue uniform, standing at attention, drawn up very erect, with a joking smile on his lips, his right hand resting loosely on the back of a large armchair, the soul of meekness, like a little saint. Bom-Crioulo guarded this miniature with religious fervour, with all the precautions of a lover, and at night, when he was going to bed, he would say goodnight to it with a wet, voluptuous kiss. He had become accustomed to doing so just as he was accustomed to making the sign of the cross before he closed his eyes. The childish superstition of a lover overflowing with tenderness. Now, however, the priceless amulet accompanied him everywhere. Even during the daytime, he would take the picture of Aleixo out of his pocket and look at it, in a state of mystical contemplation, in a confused tangle of idealised emotions, as though a ray of love, a beam of hope might come to him from that cold, inanimate piece of paper.

It seemed to him very like the original, yes, very similar. The eyes, the mouth, the smile, the nose... everything! How was it possible to copy the features of a human being like that, in just a minute? Because it was Aleixo, it was Aleixo in person!

And he felt the same amazement, he grew foolish, he lost his head, every time his eyes fell on the tiny reproduction. He would laugh sometimes, to himself, without anybody's seeing him, withdrawn in some dark corner, far from the other patients.

And every day that passed was like a year, a century, an eternity!

It occurred to him to ask someone there to write a note to the cabin-boy for him, a few words, a couple of lines.

Maybe Aleixo didn't even know where Bom-Crioulo was. He spoke to a young chap who worked in the hospital, and asked if he could do him a favour, a tiny favour. And right then and there, in the sick-room, near the window that looked out on the Organ Mountains, almost at twilight, they composed these words:

My dear Aleixo:
I don't know what's become of you, what has happened to my good, affectionate friend from our days on Misericórdia Street. It looks as though everything were over between us. I've been here, in naval hospital, going on a month now, and I hope you can come to comfort me with your presence for a few hours. I always remember our little room. Don't let me down. Come tomorrow, Sunday.
Your
Bom-Crioulo.

111

And that was all. He wanted to see what "Mr. Aleixo" would do now, whether he still cared for him, whether he was the same boy as he had known on the corvette, the same boy as he had loved on Misericórdia Street, gentle and docile, affectionate and grateful.

Early the following morning, the first sloop to leave the island for the city carried the little note, carefully folded over, written hastily, in an uneven, tortuous, illegible scrawl, by the hospital employee at twilight, by the window overlooking the sea.

The black man, anxious for a reply, became as restless as a lover in expectation of the long-awaited moment when he will embrace his beloved. He counted the hours, minute by minute, frantic at times when, by some auditory illusion, he thought he heard the boy's voice, cheerful at other moments and then completely depressed. As the hours passed, he made optimistic calculations, he mumbled incomprehensible dialogues to himself, walking back and forth along the corridors and around the hospital grounds like a madman, like a somnambulist. And if *he* didn't come? Ah, then definitely it would be because he didn't care for him, because he despised him. But at least he'd have to send an answer, come what may.

He couldn't believe that Aleixo, who had always been so kind, so good, so attentive, would just tear up the note without giving some kind of answer, a yes or a no.

He had combed his hair, he had changed clothes, and every two seconds he looked at himself in his mirror, in a miserable little broken piece of mirror, which he kept in his hammock.

Breakfast time passed, dinner time came, sailors came and went, the little bell rang announcing that new patients were arriving, the clock struck noon, and nothing at all! Not a sign of Aleixo, not a shadow of him! It was enough to drive a man crazy! If he didn't want to come, let him at least say so!

He began to lose hope. Friends! That's what happens when you trust in friends!

His inner anguish grew, his despair mounted, like a wave which swells and rises little by little, until it dissolves into foam, until it shatters on a rock. He hadn't had any breakfast, he hadn't eaten dinner, and this was the upshot of it all — Mr. Aleixo was too busy having a good time!

And when the corvettes of the fleet signalled the striking of the colours, when the great door of the hospital closed to visitors, a storm of hatred rose in the breast of that man, that man capable of utter devotion or of the most horrible violence.

Bom-Crioulo raged inwardly; his emotion was so strong that

something broke inside of him. The conviction, the absolute certainty that the boy had some other man, that he had abandoned him, had taken hold of his mind. He went back to his ward, silent, fuming with anger, in a frenzy of mute fury, burning with a fever for revenge that almost lit up his face, almost singed his flesh.

Night came, and he couldn't sleep, couldn't even close his eyes.

He tossed and turned in bed, rolling from one side to another, suffocating, without enough air for his lungs, the victim of a terrible nervous paroxysm, as though he were fighting with ghosts, at one moment pulling up the covers, at the next throwing them off, and gasping for breath, as though in the throes of an attack. Deserted! He had been deserted! Abandoned by the boy who should have loved him like a son! Abandoned by Aleixo, by his darling Aleixo!

He couldn't believe it. He had never known such despair. Only sad, gloomy thoughts and images crossed his mind. And to make things worse, to make his misery complete, all night long he heard someone moaning in the next ward — a man's voice, rough, strangled, inimitable, calling on the name of Jesus — a voice that to Bom-Crioulo sounded like his own, like the cry of an unhappy lover, appealing to God's supreme goodness. The poor wretch, whoever he was, groaned and groaned without pause, racked by horrible pains.

In the still air of the hospital there hung a very pungent smell of burnt lavender and something like the faint odour characteristic of an undertaker's parlour. Bom-Crioulo had never in his life been afraid of anything and he had always braved death fearlessly, but that night he couldn't help shivering a little with fear. There was even a moment when he became enraged at the poor sick man who was moaning. What the devil! Who could sleep with that evil omen of a sound! If he had to die, let him go ahead and die quickly.

But he repented immediately: Poor chap! He was some wretch like Bom-Crioulo himself, some poor sailor without a friend on earth.

The moaning diminished little by little, ceased little by little — a sad monody dying out in the silence of the night. In the small hours the smell of lavender still lingered, penetrating, nauseating, but the sick man had stopped moaning. Maybe he had died. Lulled by that afflicting thought, Bom-Crioulo finally fell asleep.

The clock struck three.

The next day, as it had every other day, the same thought, the same obsession, stubborn and humiliating, filled the boy-lover's soul. He himself was surprised by the way "those things" had sprung back to life — he, the man who thought he was too strong to be influenced by trifles, the man who had thought everything was easy and everything was transient in life! Because, after all, he reflected, if you love a pretty girl, a young woman, whether she's white or even coloured — what the hell! A man loses his head, and he has good reason to do so. But to go around moping, not eating, not able to sleep, not interested in anything, because of another man, because of a little pipsqueak of a boy who flirts with everybody — that's really senseless.

But it was useless for him to try to delude himself: the image of Aleixo had taken hold of his mind and tormented him more and more. It fluttered around him like some bothersome butterfly, stirring up his sexual appetite, stimulating him like some miraculous aphrodisiac, renewing all the vigour of his lusty genitals, which he had imagined had been weakened by excessive, intemperate use.

He still felt strong enough for great sexual deeds of arms, for greater and further proofs of his virility, and no human being, not even the most beautiful of women, would be able to afford him so much pleasure, so much happiness, in a single moment, as Aleixo, the delightful, incomparable cabin-boy who was now his only desire, his only ambition in the world. He had to have him, he had to enjoy him, as he had done before. It was his right. Dead or alive, one way or another, Aleixo had to belong to him!

He started thinking of a plan of escape, a way of leaving the hospital to look for the cabin-boy. Enough was enough, and the time had come now! He couldn't stand the smell of the hospital any more. He had been punished enough.

But how could he get away? How could he slip past the sentries on guard? Once he was down below, on the dock, it would be easy to get a boat for hire, or even swim across.

And the days went by, one after another, in the same uneventful fashion, monotonous, full of summer sun, and Bom-Crioulo still hadn't had a chance to put his get-away plan into effect.

He found life more and more unbearable in that "monastery of invalids". He was thin, anyone could see that — he was "a wreck", as he himself said! And the awful dreams, the nightmares! One night he dreamed that Aleixo had died, with a knife-wound in his heart. Bom-Crioulo saw the boy lying covered with blood on a canvas folding bed, naked, his lips very purple; and the Portuguese landlady, Miz Carolina, was weeping

114

like a lost soul, drying her eyes with a big kerchief of the kind you carry tobacco in. What a wild dream!

And there were other dreams, and more. If he stayed there, in that prison, he'd end up crazy, he'd like as not die a madman. Oh yes, he wanted to escape, he couldn't take it any longer. Sons of bitches!

And every day, the same thing, the same suffering, the same series of vague, incomplete ideas, the same changes of opinion, the same doubts. One night they caught him trying to climb the hospital wall.

X

Meanwhile, Aleixo was living like a prince, both on land and aboard the corvette, without a worry in the world except the duties of his rough profession. He was more at ease now, less afraid that Bom-Crioulo would come looking for him, seeking revenge, and he became more and more intimate with the landlady, going so far as to forget completely certain things that had made him timid and fearful. He was husky, strong, healthy, much more of a man than before, despite his tender years. His muscles were as well-developed as those of an acrobat, his blue eyes were penetrating, his face was broad and sunburnt. In a short period of time he had taken on an admirable appearance of physical vigour, and had become even more handsome and popular. As for the Portuguese landlady, she lived for him: she loved him, she adored him.

Ah! She was ready and willing, she was, to do anything for her "little bitty pretty one"! When Aleixo came ashore, he had everything he could ask for in that shabby house on Misericórdia Street. She kept everything in stock for her handsome young sailor: fruit, candies, special foods, Portuguese-type delicacies, this, that and the other thing. She herself washed and ironed his clothes with the scrupulous affection of a loving mother, folding his shirts, perfuming them with rosemary so that he could change when he came from work. How things had changed in that house since the black man moved out! The attic, the mysterious attic, was abandoned now. Aleixo didn't even want to know of its existence. He hated it, because it was there that he had become a slave to Bom-Crioulo; it was there that he had "lost all shame". The poor room was like a place that had been put under a curse: it was always locked and bolted, sad and dusty. Miz Carolina seldom opened it — only when she had to stick some old piece of furniture or some useless belonging in there. The picture of the emperor, the canvas folding bed, the furnishings and decorations supplied by Bom-Crioulo and the cabin-boy, everything that had previously been the pride and joy of the two friends, had long since disappeared. Nothing remained now of that life lived there together.

"And what if the nigger comes by here some fine day?" worried Aleixo, apprehensively.

"What d'you mean, 'come by here'? He won't come by!" said the landlady, with a gesture of profound conviction. "Bom-Crioulo doesn't even remember who you are any more. He's drinking and fighting and whoring around. All he wanted was to take advantage of you."

Then she added:

"If he *should* come by, it doesn't matter. A little lie never hurt anybody. I'll say the city engineering department won't let anybody live in the attic, because the roof might cave in. I'll invent some story."

And Aleixo's belongings — only Aleixo's — were moved down to the landlady's bedroom, on the second floor. From that point on, they started sleeping together, like a married couple, in her big double bed. And nobody entered the little attic room any more; it was turned into a storeroom for old furniture, dust-covered, insect-ridden, rat-haunted.

This arrangement had been going on for nearly a month, and, far from being bored, Aleixo felt, on the contrary, a deep, firm affection for Miz Carolina. He even asked her not to have anything more to do with the bearded butcher. He wanted to have her for himself, all for himself, or it was all over between them!

She tried to convince him that Man'el, the butcher, was a necessary evil, because he gave her a monthly allowance, because he paid the rent on the house: he was a gold mine! As for the man himself, well, that was another story! Her "bitty pretty one" could rest easy: there was no danger. Man'el was a poor devil, a weakling, a dirty swine.

But Aleixo got angry. No, ma'am, he would not accept the presence of another man! She could very well work like an honest woman and earn money to pay the rent. No, ma'am: it was Aleixo or the butcher.

Miz Carolina laughed and promised she would not let Man'el visit her any more. They would live "decently"!

Aleixo was very happy, very proud of himself, very confident in her.

But the truth is that if the butcher had not kept on sending meat and paying the rent on the house, both Aleixo and the landlady would have had to end their love affair.

"Man'el doesn't know anything about my 'bitty pretty one', and *he* doesn't know anything about Man'el", reflected Miz Carolina.

And everything went on without a hitch — a golden boat on a sea of roses.

Until the letter from the black man arrived: "My dear Aleixo..."

Miz Carolina ran her eyes greedily over the paper till she reached the signature, and when she saw the name of Bom-Crioulo she shook her head disgustedly. Then she re-read those words impregnated with love and longing, and she remained a long time, standing, in the middle of the room, as though she had lost her reason.

It was about eleven o'clock — a hot December morning of light and dust.

She had just finished her usual breakfast of beefsteak and *café au lait* when the knock came at the door.

It was the note from the black man, that "devil"!

Aleixo had gone aboard that morning and wasn't due to return till the next day. Fortunately, dear God, fortunately, her "bitty pretty one" wasn't in the house at the time, because if he read the note, he might be influenced.

She looked over the page once again, as though she were trying to memorise it, and then she tore it into little pieces and threw them into the garbage can.

And that was that! That letter was of no value anyhow!

But she kept on thinking about the matter, seized by a vague, mysterious presentiment that made her heart beat faster. Horrible ideas of crimes, murders and bloodshed assailed her; she remembered affairs that had caused great excitement in Rio de Janeiro, cases of jealousy and betrayal. In Senhor dos Passos Street[1] a sergeant had knifed a poor prostitute to death, because he'd caught her out with another man. The police had come running to the scene, but it was night, and the killer got away, leaving the body of the girl covered with knife-wounds and red with blood. She remembered another terrible case: it had been on Arcos Street;[2] the murderer had cut the woman into pieces, like someone slaughtering a cow. The populace had come running in crowds to witness the spectacle. It was rumoured that the victim was an upper-class Spanish girl called Lola.

All these memories thronged in disorderly fashion through her mind, chilling her love, filling her with apprehensions, with childish fears, like an omen of approaching misfortune.

---

[1] A street in the business centre of downtown Rio de Janeiro.
[2] A street in the "bohemian" district of downtown Rio de Janeiro, known as Lapa, near the city's ancient aqueduct, Os Arcos.

She spent the day doing nothing, troubled in spirit, sometimes in her room, lying down, thinking, calculating the future,
reminiscing over one thing or another, sighing for the good old
days of her youth, sometimes downstairs in the yard, walking
back and forth like a crazy woman: "This heat in December is
just unbearable, ugh!"

She was mightily surprised when she heard the clock strike
two: "Just two! Dear God, what a long day!" And she had no
clothes to wash, no work to do, nothing to distract her. That
was contrary to her way of living: she couldn't be up and about
without doing something. What a nuisance!

She couldn't take her mind off the black man's note, which
she had torn up. So Bom-Crioulo *still* remembered Aleixo! The
big fag! She had never imagined that a love affair between two
men could last so long and be so persistent! And a Negro at that,
good Lord, an immoral, loathsome nigger like that!

Night came, and her spirit remained troubled, with the same
vague, indefinite apprehension. She was almost sorry she had
taken up with Aleixo. She had been leading such a quiet life in
her little nook on Misericórdia Street, living as she wanted to,
without any problems. After all, the cabin-boy was a mere child,
and she was a middle-aged woman.

And then she reconsidered: Ah! But nobody's free in this life.
A man and a woman are like fire and gunpowder. Even at nearly
forty years of age, she was still a woman, she had blood in her
veins and a heart made for loving.

She closed all the doors, more carefully than ever, she
checked the yard, and she went to bed very early, thinking about
Bom-Crioulo, Aleixo and the crazy things human beings do. She
heard the trolleys roll by almost all night long. The air was as
hot and sultry as an oven, and she couldn't get any rest, she
couldn't fall peacefully asleep; in vain would she close her eyes,
only to open them again in the same instant, suffocated, upset
by ridiculous nervous scruples typical of some hysterical
weakling and not of a woman like her, plump, strong and
healthy!

She couldn't find any position in bed that suited her: she
suffered from a sense of indisposition, a kind of asthma that
deprived her of both breath and sleep. It was the first time that
anything like this had happened to her. She threw her bedroom
doors wide open — both the door that opened on the dining-
room and the one that led to the hallway, but it was useless —
the same lack of air, the same hellish heat. And always the
memory of the black man and the cabin-boy tormented her, like

119

a cruel nightmare. She saw Bom-Crioulo coming into the house drunk, his eyes ablaze, a sailor's knife in his hand, brandishing the weapon, mad with hatred, fierce, terrible, foul-smelling, and, suddenly, falling on the cabin-boy, foaming with jealousy, lacing him with knife-wounds. And she seemed to see the body tumble to the ground without a word, in a river of blood, dead! And then the police, cries for help, public shame and exposure, spectators who had come to *see*.

The clock struck two in the morning. There were no more trolley-cars. The street was completely silent, and within the house the same noiseless suffocating torpor reigned — the infinite calm of some subterranean dwelling.

A quarter of an hour later, the landlady fell into a deep, leaden sleep — a sleep as heavy and immobile as the sleep eternal.

As usual, Aleixo was off duty the next day, and, as usual, he went straight to the house, light-hearted, carefree, in his blue uniform, with a white ribbon on his sailor's cap, cheerful, smelling of cologne. Miz Carolina was in the kitchen, preparing the meal. It was three in the afternoon. The boy was surprised to find the street-door closed at that hour, and he knocked hard. This was something new!

The landlady ran immediately to the window to see. Could it be her "bitty pretty one?"

There was a slight stir in the neighbourhood. Down below, on the ground floor, a black head stuck itself out, full of curiosity, pretending it had come to the window just at that moment quite naturally, by accident. The counter boy in the bakery across the way craned his neck, from behind the counter.

As soon as she recognised the sailor-boy, Miz Carolina came and opened the door, with an exclamation of surprise: she hadn't expected him so early!

"Early? D'you think it's still early? That's a good one: it's almost nighttime!"

"Oh, no, my boy, it's two o'clock!"

"No, ma'am, sorry; it's going on four o'clock."

And they climbed the stairs. She had her arm on the boy's shoulder, but he walked up with a very serious, suspicious air, his eyes lowered and a crestfallen expression on his youthful face. What a way of putting him in his place, closing the downstairs door at that hour!

And the landlady answered, as she kissed him on the cheek:

"Don't be angry, my little jasmin flower, don't be angry. A closed door keeps temptations away. I just got a strange feeling, I felt afraid."

"Temptations, afraid, be damned! You aren't any baby to go running and hiding like that. It just makes people wonder."

But Miz Carolina didn't want to tell him the truth, and confess her fears of Bom-Crioulo, or tell him the story of the note. Why upset Aleixo? He knew perfectly well that the black man would not give him up just like that. Negroes are a devilish race, a cursed lot; they never forgive, they never forget. Aleixo was quite familiar with Bom-Crioulo's temperament. Besides, the whole business of the note was a piece of nonsense that it wasn't worth thinking about: nigger business.

"Listen, my little one, I swear to you that I'll never shut the downstairs door again. Calm down, will you? Calm down."

They were in the bedroom. The cabin-boy's gaze examined in turn the furniture, the bed, the room, the dining-room, as if he were trying to discover visible signs of her infidelity. The woman helped him undress, recommending a thousand precautions so that he should not catch cold. "Listen, change your shirt; look, drink a little brandy; be careful of draughts; put on these slippers."

He had never witnessed such affection, such devotion. The landlady redoubled her attentions to him, with demonstrations of almost childish tenderness. She even wanted him to mistreat her, to humiliate her. Aleixo's blue eyes exerted a strange power over her, an irresistible fascination: they penetrated deep into her soul and controlled her, turning her into a poor weak-willed animal; they burned her like a burning coal, spurring her on to any kind of self-sacrifice. When she was with him, she lost all fear, all doubt; she would have been willing to attack a man, to be stabbed to death, to kill, to commit any act, however insane.

Today above all, unlike the previous night, when she had fallen victim to her fears and had wanted to be free of the boy, today above all, she was overflowing with an almost maternal kindness. Her love had become a kind of fanatical worship, a religious devotion. She kissed and kissed him, meek, caressing and content, as though all virtues were to be found there, in Aleixo's blue eyes, in that ideal gaze, infinitely sweet and gentle.

"You're my saint, my little one," she would say. "You're my only happiness in this old world, in this vale of tears."

And she'd hug him, nibbling him with her teeth, nervous, excited, offering herself to the youth in a fury of morbidity and sensuality.

"What the devil is going on, woman, have you gone crazy?" the cabin-boy scolded. Since he had arrived, he hadn't once opened up in a friendly smile. "What's happened to upset you so much?"

"Oh! But I love you so much, my darling baby, I love you so much!"

He said nothing. Dinner was eaten in the same atmosphere of cold formality. Miz Carolina in turn became distant and unresponsive, humiliated by Aleixo's treatment of her. Dry and indifferent, he made not the slightest effort to please. They both sat in silence, like two strangers at a hotel table. But finally she couldn't endure the uncomfortable silence any longer.

"What have I done to you, my baby, tell me, what have I done wrong? Wasn't I at home alone when you came, working, drudging away? What have I done?"

Aleixo remained silent, his lips trembling convulsively, his eyes fixed on the wall.

"Come on, tell me, what have I done wrong?" the landlady insisted, touching his arm. "You must have some reason for getting so angry."

But he didn't move, he didn't answer. He sat there, impenetrable in his cruel, stubborn muteness, which had reduced the poor woman almost to tears. At this point, Miz Carolina felt desperate, and, getting up sadly, she went to her bedroom, cursing her luck, bewailing her "misfortune." She was an unlucky, wretched woman, everybody looked down on her, she was tired of suffering, life was hell, she'd rather die!

And she kept repeating mournfully:

"What have I done, dear Lord, what have I ever done to that man?"

Aleixo felt a stirring of pity and, getting up also, went to the bedroom.

"Then why did you close the downstairs door?" he said. "Is something mysterious going on in this house? Didn't you expect me today?"

"Oh, my boy, didn't I already tell you that I closed it because I just suddenly felt afraid?"

"Afraid, afraid, what nonsense, woman! I can forgive anything. But you're acting very badly."

Miz Carolina had stretched out on the bed and was sniffling, drying her tears with her apron, lamenting her lot in life.

"Why did you suddenly feel afraid today? Don't you leave the door open every day, don't you usually leave it wide open?"

"You're making a big scene over nothing, over a matter of no importance. Either a man trusts a woman or he doesn't. You've never caught me with anybody else, for you to have such a bad opinion of me."

"All right, but be truthful, then, and explain what happened.

Why did you close the downstairs door?"

That was the beginning of making up. Aleixo had approached the bed, moved by the grieving voice of the woman, who was looking at him now with tender eyes, full of humility and resignation.

"D'you really want me to tell you why I closed the downstairs door? Then sit down here, and I'll tell you. It was for your sake that I didn't say anything; I didn't want you to worry."

The cabin-boy's mind imagined a whole series of unpleasant things: attempted break-ins, threats of prison, violence, and horrible things like that! Bom-Crioulo, however, was far from his thoughts. For him, the black man had simply died, he had disappeared. He had never heard anything more about him from anyone; he definitely would never come back; maybe he was sailing, on the high seas, on some long trip.

And the landlady recounted the story of the note, which she had torn up, because it wasn't worthwhile getting upset about it.

Aleixo listened with great interest, chin in hand, leaning forward on the wide bed.

"And where is he now?" he asked, with lively curiosity.

"In naval hospital, on the island; he's sick with something. If you didn't know him, you might believe such a story."

Aleixo didn't want to say anything, but the story of the note had touched him, had filled him with a vague sadness: Bom-Crioulo still remembered him!

He thought he should visit the black man; it might be the wisest thing.

"What do you think?"

Miz Carolina disapproved: "Good Lord, no, what nonsense! That would be like jumping off Corcovado Mountain. No, never!"

And she added: "Let him be, my boy. Little by little he'll forget you. Live your own life and leave him in peace. We're doing very nicely without him. Never!"

"And if he comes here some fine day?"

"What? That's why I have the downstairs door closed."

"Well," murmured the cabin-boy, getting up. "That's life!"

"And no one can go against the laws of Providence," summed up Miz Carolina, dogmatically.

The little quarrel was over. Everything had been explained. Aleixo had admitted how unjust he had been to the landlady, and she had forgiven him, kind as always, generous as always. Laughing, happy, cuddling against each other, they watched the passers-by on the street from the bedroom window. Who cared about Bom-Crioulo? Who cared about yellow fever?[1] In all Rio de Janeiro, in the whole world, there were only two happy people: the cabin-boy and the Portuguese landlady — happy as Adam and Eve before they knew sin, happy as every pair of lovers is happy.

They went out together for a stroll that night. Aleixo suggested they should go to the Passeio Público and have a dish of ice cream, or a cold fruit drink, or anything to drink. You couldn't stay indoors in such heat! Miz Carolina mentioned the Guarda-Velha.[2] Wouldn't it be better to go to the Guarda-Velha, to the brewery there? They had music, too.

But the cabin-boy pointed out that they'd be very much in the public eye at the Guarda-Velha; a lot of sailors from aboard ship went there; there were too many people. The Passeio Público was bigger and not so crowded; they'd have more freedom there. And to get there, they just had to take the Lapa[3] trolley-car.

"Oh! Go in your sailor's uniform," implored Miz Carolina, when she saw him putting on a sports jacket. "It's cooler, and it makes people respect you."

"Clothing isn't what inspires respect," replied Aleixo sententiously, as he buttoned the jacket. "It's good behaviour that inspires respect. Let me have a little change every now and then!"

She loved so much to see him in his uniform, "so little and cute," like a painting, attracting everybody's attention, admired, envied, praised. His sailor's uniform really looked far better on him: there was no comparison! What was a soldier in civilian clothing? A man like anybody else, a poor devil who didn't inspire any special respect. But in uniform!

"But I don't want to, woman, I don't want to. These are things that . . ."

"All right, no need to quarrel. Go as you please."

It was getting dark. Objects could no longer be distinguished clearly inside the house. Outside, on the street, the first gas-lamps were lit, and it was very quiet: a deep somnolence reigned in the neighbourhood.

---

[1] Yellow fever was endemic in Rio de Janeiro until the hygienic reforms of the epidemiologist Oswaldo Cruz, at the beginning of this century.
[2] This was a police post on the present Senador Dantas Street (then called Guarda-Velha Street), in downtown Rio de Janeiro.
[3] A former "bohemian" district of downtown Rio de Janeiro, now largely destroyed by urban reform, once notable for its mundane and literary life. The Passeio Público is located very close to it.

I think it's going to rain, said Aleixo, stepping over to the window.

Actually, dark clouds were spreading across the sky, low, heavy clouds, billowing like the black smoke from a fire. The air was getting cooler. A gentle, caressing breeze was even blowing. A man's voice could be heard, imitating a train whistle, somewhere near Misericórdia Hospital.

The Lapa trolley-car was passing. Miz Carolina and Aleixo boarded it. She looked happy and enthusiastic in her improvised *toilette*, which gave her an honest, good-natured appearance. He looked a little sad, standing upright and circumspect, with his straw hat thrust back on his head, showing his hair slicked down with hair cream, and the blood-red tie he had put on.

And the trolley-car took off.

XI

A dull despair, an unbelievably profound, fantastic despair, filled Bom-Crioulo's embittered heart. It was complicated by pathological causes, aggravated by a kind of contagious leprosy that had quickly sprouted all over his body, on which the pale marks of the caning he had received were still stubbornly bleeding. He no longer retained any hope that Aleixo would come to the hospital to visit him; his eyes had been opened. The cabin-boy had abandoned him; he had forgotten him, and he hadn't even explained why! Troubles just attract more troubles. In the final analysis, a person had to turn bad and do wrong things. This idea of planning your life, of making sacrifices for other people, of behaving decently, wasn't worth anything; it was all nonsense, all stupidity.

He had his calm moments, when he tried to put all ideas of revenge, of seeking satisfaction, out of his mind, like someone who considers himself superior to the little tragedies of life. During the daytime, he would play checkers with the hosptial employee who had written the note for him, resigned, even-tempered, even jolly on occasion. But he never lost, even then, the vague expression of sadness that always floated in his eyes, revealing mysterious depths of the soul.

It was at night, though, that the problem of Aleixo came back to his mind, filling his head with ghosts, peopling it with dreams, with the insistency of regret — at night, in the hours of sleep, when all was still in the old hospital.

He simply could not accept the idea that Aleixo had abandoned him for someone else. And who was this "someone else?" Some other sailor, naturally, probably a first-class man. What ingratitude, what baseness! To abandon him, just like that, and why? Because he was black, because he had been a slave? He was just as good a man as the emperor!

He wore himself out in childish ruminations, commenting on Aleixo's behaviour, howling curses that no one heard, sending out lightning-bolts of anger, stormy and frightful in his hallucinated silence. Those were nights — night after night — of exhausting, fantasy-ridden sleeplessness, of a crude but over-powering obsession. And when he finally felt sleepy, in the early morning hours, it was impossible to sleep, because then he also began to feel what he called "the mange," a horrid itching in his skin, in his whole body, as though his blood were about to spurt out through every pore in a terrible hemorrhage, or as if he were being pricked with pins and needles from head to toe. He couldn't close his eyes or calm his mind. His only desire, on such occasions, was to go running outside like a madman, jump into a cold bath, and squat completely naked in the water for as long as possible. It seemed as if a curse had fallen on him! Sores broke out all over his body: he had a huge, open, running one on his left knee. He couldn't understand it all. Some undeserved curse that had been laid on him, perhaps. It was ghastly! For a man to spend the whole night without sleeping, thinking of this and that and the other thing, and, to top it all off, that devilish itch that was enough to drive anybody crazy!

It was at those moments that he was angry with Aleixo, it was then that he raged against the cabin-boy as "the cause of all his problems." In that suffering, despairing state of both body and mind, he completely lost his reason. He had only one idea in his head — to revenge himself on the boy, to pursue him to his death, to annihilate him forever!

What he felt in those moments was a mixture of hatred, love and jealousy. The desire to have the cabin-boy, to enjoy him again, far from dying out, merely increased in his heart, wounded by the youth's rejection of him. Aleixo was a lost terrain which he had to regain, come what may. No one had the right to rob him of that friendship, that treasury of delights, that tower of ivory which he had built with his own hands. Aleixo was his, he belonged to him by right, like some irremovable piece of personal property. And from the desire was born also his hatred of the cabin-boy, a hatred as unheeding, as brutal, as deeply meditated as the wrath of Othello.[1].

Aleixo with another man! The very idea made him crazy with jealousy; it tortured him like a physical pain, like a pulsing, open wound.

But how happy he felt, how relieved, how supremely fortunate, when at last, in the morning, clear daylight by now, the sun, warm and lively, entered wrapped in mystery into the sick-ward, and life, beautiful life, began its daily round again in the whole hospital!

---

[1] Considering the obvious literary debt that *Bom-Crioulo* owes to *Othello*, it's interesting that this is the only direct reference to the play.

It was on one of these nights of obsession and despair that Bom-Crioulo climbed down the wall of the hospital and set off on a bee-line for Misericórdia Street, blindly, carelessly, like someone about to jump over a cliff.

It was a Saturday and a holiday. Among the sailors who'd come to the hospital to visit friends, Bom-Crioulo recognised the Drip, from the corvette, his former colleague — the Drip, Herculano, who had been caught practising an ugly and depressing but very human act, up against the main rail, in the prow, on a certain night.

"Herculano, come on over here!"

"Oh, Bom-Crioulo!"

"So what have you been doing?" asked the black man, with a purpose of his own in mind, leading the other sailor by the arm. "Where are you now?"

Herculano had changed; he was no longer the same Drip, reserved and friendless, with great dark circles under his eyes, speaking hesitantly and slowly. He was different, admirably different now — robust, rosy-cheeked, his eyes bright and sparkling, without any melancholy or any shadow of sadness in his expression. He had lost the pallor that had given him such a miserable, insignificant appearance; he talked smoothly now, in a loud voice, and laughed, like a child, over nothing at all.

"Where am I now? On the corvette, still on the corvette."

"Still?" said Bom-Crioulo, apparently surprised, concealing the satisfaction that this answer afforded him. "My God, you're still on the corvette, man?"

"Why not? That's a *real* ship. Since it came out of dry dock it doesn't even look like the same ship. It does your heart good to see it. It's all freshly painted, all renovated, it looks like one of those models of ships they make."

"But how did you do it? How did you change so much, lad? You used to be so weak and pale, and now you're looking really handsome, man!"

"Handsome nothing!" smiled Herculano. "I've weighed even more than I do now."

He was observing Bom-Crioulo. The black man looked so weak, so worn-out! You could see the bones of his face, and he had a great scar, a sort of deep furrow, in his neck.

"Are you sick?" he asked.

"I've got some kind of itch, and sores all over my body. They say it's the mange."

"Aha! Because you're thin, old chap, you're nothing but skin and bones. What the hell!"

And after a pause, he added:

"I came to see Anacleto; he's here with V.D. I didn't know that you were sick here too, that you were in here. I thought you'd be far away from here."

"That's right, I've been here for nearly a month, in this damned place, just wasting away!"

They reached the infirmary. The patients glanced at them, and continued chatting in groups, in the corridors, on the hospital grounds. Some convalescents were playing *peteca*[1] in a little square from which you could catch sight of the sea.

It was going on six o'clock. The warships, motionless and flag-bedecked, gave the scene a festive air. Bugle-calls could be heard in the distance, and sounds of music came from the mainland, from the city. Ferries to and from Niterói crossed one another's paths in the middle of the quiet bay. Everywhere, on land and sea, there was a tremor of universal happiness, holiday happiness, a strange eagerness that dissolved in the distance, into the first mists of twilight. The sun was no longer visible; its brightness little by little was becoming diffuse, faint, languishing, like a misty morning. The silhouettes of the ships, the outlines of mountain, tower and factory chimney — all were vanishing into the night which slowly fell, alive with mystery.

Herculano was not concerned that night was approaching, because he was on leave; from the island, he could take a boat across to the city. But he couldn't stay long, because they'd close the main door of the hospital soon, and he didn't want to have to spend the night in that "living cemetery."

Bom-Crioulo reassured him: "It's still early, man. What's the rush, what's the hurry?"

Skillfully, amiably, he added:

"Sit down a while. Don't be so bashful; everything here belongs to you and to me and to the government. Sit down: we can talk more easily."

Herculano's gaze swept around the sick-room: floor, ceiling, beds ranged in a row: all in all, it wasn't such a bad life — good beds, good food, freedom.

"That's what *you* say, because you haven't spent a night inside here yet, old chap. This is a real hell. It's only fit for somebody who has no place else to go. What we have on board ship, that's comfortable beds for you."

---

[1] A badminton-like Brazilian game, played with a small, light rubber or leather ball, covered with feathers, which is thrust into the air with the palm of the hand.

"Can I smoke?" asked the sailor.

"It's against regulations, but light up your cigarette."

They'd sat down on the black man's very dirty bed. Just for a second, warned Herculano.

And Bom-Crioulo launched into conversation:

"Tell me about everybody, Herculano. How is Aleixo, how is Agostinho the guard, how is everybody?"

"All right. Agostinho the guard is as nasty as he always was, that son-of-a-bitch — nasty and always trying to get a fellow in trouble. Luckily, I haven't fallen into his clutches, luckily, I say! Aleixo, just between you and me, is in very thick with the officers. He practically lives in the gunroom. He's the one who winds the ship's clock; he cleans up the officers' cabins; he does everything. He's a clown, my boy, just a big clown; he's everybody's spoiled baby on board. He comes when he pleases, he goes when he pleases."

Bom-Crioulo cleared his throat.

"Me, I don't talk to him any more," continued Herculano. "We're not on speaking terms, because of some silly nonsense, some tomfoolery. The other day we almost had a fight. They even say he's got a girl on shore."

"He's got a girl?"

"Yes, he's living with a girl, a little coxcomb like him. That's what they say; I don't know."

Bom-Crioulo was beginning to understand now; he was very alert, controlling himself, keeping down the flood of obscenities and profanities, the wave of anger which was on the point of erupting from his mouth. He was in agony. In the warm semi-darkness of the sick-ward his eyes took on a damp, wounded expression, like the look of a shipwrecked person lost in the infinite circle of the ocean. It was a muffled, impenetrable storm that was raging in him, the crumbling of all his beliefs, all his illusions, all the forces that help maintain the balance of a human being's nature when it is tried beyond its endurance.

"Sant'ana deserted, he ran away, nobody knows where he went. Poor chap, he took a lot of canings; you'd think he was an ox the way they beat him! He was a poor devil."

And they talked a little while longer. Talkative, chatty, Herculano told detailed stories of life on board. And finally, when night had come, he said:

"Well, good-bye, Bom-Crioulo, I'm moving on now. I hope you get better, eh? I hope you'll be completely cured soon. If you need me for anything, I'm there on the corvette. Good night!"

"Good night," murmured the black man, in a deep, sad,

almost funereal voice. And the stars came out one by one in the high, clear, autumn sky.

Bom-Crioulo, overflowing as he was with hatred and despair, couldn't even think of sleeping. Like a death-knell, those brutally truthful words still echoed in his ears, in all their pungent coarseness: "They even say he's living with a girl!"

Aleixo living with a girl! Living with a girl, the boy who had been all his, the boy who had belonged to him like his own heart, the boy who had never talked to him about sex, who had been so innocent, so devoted, so good before! Living with a girl, feeling the contact of another body that was not Bom-Crioulo's, letting himself be kissed and bitten, in the throes of orgasm, by another person who was not Bom-Crioulo!

And now he really felt a tremendous desire, a mad longing to see the boy lying, defeated, at his feet, like some small animal. Now he really felt, renewed in him, those greedy instincts of a steer set loose among cows, the irresponsibility of a male animal in heat, the nostalgia of an excited libertine. Herculano's words (the story that the cabin-boy was living with a girl) had stirred his blood, had been a kind of wild nettle that pricked his skin, rousing him, infuriating him with desire. Now he was really going to assert his rights! And it wasn't just a matter of having the boy, of enjoying him as he had done before, up there in the little room on Misericórdia Street — now he was going to have his pleasure with him by hurting him, seeing him suffer, by hearing him moan with pain. No, it was not merely the simple pleasure of orgasm, the normal sensation that he desired after having heard Herculano's words: it was brutal, painful pleasure, beyond all laws, beyond all inhibitions. And he was going to have it, whatever the price he had to pay!

Definitely, he was going to put his plan of escape into effect that very night; he would roam the world looking for Aleixo.

Disturbed, overwrought and nervous, he sat down to think. The cabin-boy appeared to him now in a new light, transformed by his amatory excesses, debauched, having lost that innocent air that everyone admired in him. He imagined the boy with lean, sharp features now, blotched with pimples, thin, colourless, his lips pale and bloodless. Small wonder! A man can't take too much of it — and a mere child! Aleixo would probably be completely worn-out, used-up. He saw him in the arms of his girl, his lover — the adolescent boy, the young girl in all the freshness of her twenty years of age; he saw Aleixo writhing in unspeakably pleasurable spasms, his body glued to hers, on a cool, white bed; he saw him writhe and fall back, exhausted, crucified on the cross of pleasure, mortally weak. Then the girl would bend over him and join her mouth to his in a deep kiss of gratitude. And the next day, the next night, the scene would repeat.

Bom-Crioulo's mind was wandering. The train of unconscious associations led him into a universe of vague ideas, where he couldn't decide on any quick, conclusive course of action. Only one idea remained firm and clear in his mind: running away, escaping as soon as possible, not waiting a second more, breaking through the walls of his isolation and greeting the new day in the streets of the city, far from the hospital — "that shitty hospital!"

His plan couldn't fail. He would leave the window open — because of the heat, he'd say. He'd pack his things — what things? he didn't need to pack anything! — and late at night he'd climb down by a rope. The windows that looked out on the Organ Mountains were right above a somewhat irregular terrain, a kind of rugged slope, rather steep, which ran headlong down toward various repair shops and small shipyards that were installed there on the island. But the windows were not so high that it would be impossible to climb down from them, though it would be difficult and would require agility. And Bom-Crioulo would not be the first; others, before him, had escaped that way. There was the story of one chap who had rolled all the way down the hill. They found him half-dead at the foot of a tree, his body covered with bruises, blood gushing from his nose; he died of the fall, of some serious illness he'd contracted in his spinal column.

But the black man didn't hesitate. He got up (it was one in the morning), he went to the toilet, so that nobody could see what he was doing, he tied in his waistband the sailor's knife that he always carried, he put on his sailor shirt under his white hospital uniform, and he came back cautiously to the ward, listening to the silence, scrutinising the darkness. And then, it was all done very quickly. He wound the rope — a thick, braided rope — around the window and — sons of bitches! — he climbed down and landed. The bay was fearfully dark, and it was so quiet it would make a man's hair stand on end. It was the hour of deep, profound sleep. From one minute to the next the sentries would cry out their call of "on guard!", prolonging the syllables; and echoes on land and sea repeated the call. There was no other voice, no other sign of life. The brightly illuminated city, twinkling with microscopic dots of light, was like a vast city of the dead in the melancholy stillness of the night.

Bom-Crioulo felt a mild chill, a light morning breeze that made the skin on the nape of his neck crawl. Touching with his hands, feeling his way, he followed along, parallel to the hospital wall, without looking back, unable to see anything. He'd examined the terrain carefully before he set out on his adventure; this way, going in this direction, he would be walking straight toward a slope that was not very difficult to negotiate. The dry dock was right below him. He had to be very careful, very agile, so as not to fall into it. He inched along and inched along, sometimes squatting down, sometimes standing up, holding on here, holding on there, groping, and finally — sons of bitches! — he reached the dock, at the water's edge, without even a scratch on him. The half-hour was striking in the Candelária church[1] bell-tower — a full, sonorous peal, that resounded dully in the distance, awakening echoes. "I still have to cross the canal," said Bom-Crioulo to himself, as he measured visually the expanse of water separating the island from the War Arsenal. "Just be patient, just be patient a bit. Easy does it..." He squeezed his whole body behind a crane, and sat and thought. He'd go straight to the house on Misericórdia Street. He wanted to see what was going on; he wanted to give Mr. Aleixo a little surprise. And what about the Portuguese landlady? He had forgotten about her! Yes, of course, could it be the landlady?

Like a bolt of lightning, a suspicion flashed through his mind, dazzling him: What? No! It couldn't be! What nonsense!

The chill increased. The Candelária church clock, deep and full-voiced, struck two. Bom-Crioulo raised his eyes to the heavens. The stars were throbbing; the Milky Way, white and sinuous, shone in the infinite quiet of the night. Opposite him, at the arsenal, the silhouette of a great, dark chimney reared against the sky. The water slapped monotonously against the dock, in its endless ebb and flow. "On guard!" shouted the sentries constantly, on the island, at the arsenal, in the warehouses. Everywhere the same silence, the same quiet, the same profound calm reigned.

It seemed as if the night would never finish, never come to an end; it was like eternity. Pulled by the tide, an object was floating slowly downstream. An old piece of clothing, a rag, thought the black man. Who knows? Maybe it was a body.

---

[1] A church in downtown Rio de Janeiro, located at present at the top of Presidente Vargas Avenue.

And it didn't get lighter, and dawn didn't come. He was beginning to grow impatient. What the devil was he doing sitting there, without making a decision? Was that why he'd escaped, to sit there with his mouth open, falling asleep as he waited? But the only solution was to wait; there was nothing else to do. Swim across? What? With the sentries there? Patience, patience...

Three o'clock in the Candelária church bell-tower. Only a single voice called out, distant and lonely: "On guard!" There was no echo.

Bom-Crioulo leaned his head against the crane, drunk with sleep, his eyelids like lead, his whole body cramped and uncomfortable, and in spite of "the itch", which was crawling up his legs now, like an ant-hill, he fell asleep to the sound of water lapping against the dock.

When he opened his eyes, minutes later, it was almost daylight. The uproar of sloops and boatmen around the Customs House docks was beginning. You could hear the slap of oars and the puff of a launch letting off steam. The Organ Mountains, still indistinct in the half-light of dawn, little by little were beginning to display the lovely shape of the gigantic musical instrument that gave them their name. A few pallid lights shone in the great amphitheatre of the city. The street-lights had been turned off. Since three o'clock a little bell had been ringing insistently, nasally, from the Benedictine monastery, calling to matins, like the joyous chiming of some small village church bell proclaiming the triumphs of Christianity. On the battleships of the bay, buglers were rehearsing the notes of morning reveille. On the other side of the bay, in Niterói, a fine, transparent mist, like the emanations from some great lake, cloaked the mountains, hiding the landscape from one end to the other. And out beyond the harbour bar, beyond Sugar Loaf, a rose-coloured streak was growing ever brighter, ever more dazzling in the pale sky.

Bom-Crioulo looked all around him, surprised, astonished, as if he had found himself in some unknown place. The first word that came to his lips was an obscenity: sons of bitches! He was going to get caught! To work, to work! Luckily, it wasn't broad daylight yet.

Not a boat, not a skiff of any kind was near there in the canal. All the activity was around the Customs House, at the Mineiros dock. War sloops passed by: Bom-Crioulo hid, so as not to be spotted by them — Damn! Damn! And all for the sake of a miserable cabin-boy!

Suddenly he heard the sound of oars in water, He came closer: it was a boat for hire. At last! At last!

The tiny skiff that was heading for the island had no awning for protection from the sun. Rowing it was a bewhiskered old Portuguese. To stern, on the back seat, the boat bore the name *Luís de Camões*, written above a painting done in oils, which might have been the great epic poet, or any other bearded individual. A crown of laurel leaves had been painted on his forehead. In this wretched daubing, it was the poet's *left* eye [1] which was an empty socket — a fact which, in the final analysis, was of no concern to Bom-Crioulo.

"Will you take me to the dock?" the black man asked the Portuguese.

"Straightway!" said the old man, pulling up. "The *Luís de Camões* never sleeps."

"Let's go."

"You may board now."

"Oops!"

And with a jump, Bom-Crioulo was on board. He was finally free from danger. "Sons of bitches!"

And from that moment on, he disappeared into the labyrinth of the city, walking with his long, nimble stride, turning into streets, cutting corners, "veering and tacking."

It was a marvellous, marvellous day! A day when the sky and the mountains seemed to have put on their most beautiful hues — a day of freedom!

---

[1] The great Portuguese epic poet, Luís de Camões (1524-1580), was blind in his *right* eye.

XII

Hardly any movement in Misericórdia Street yet. Badly-dressed men, workmen and day-labourers, came down the street with the stupefied, miserable air of tame sheep trotting along slowly, fatalistically, with tired lassitude, almost the indolence of eunuchs. A milk cow, with great heavy teats and a bell around its neck, went its daily round, docile and swollen-bellied, a string of spittle running from its snout in threads of foam. The blue-painted garbage cart went about its morning tasks, stopping here and there.

Not a spark of life broke the monotony of the neighbourhood — only the sound of the trolleys and an occasional raised voice. A strong odour of urine hung everywhere, like the aggressive aroma of some public washroom, poisoning the air, making breathing difficult. The first rays of the sun struck windows obliquely, waking up those who lived inside, colouring the façades of houses with strokes of gold, making the granite trim of doorways glitter like pure crystal, dazzling the eyes like the hot flashes of street-lamps. And already you could feel a mild heat, a lukewarm putrefaction, the beginnings of sultriness.

Cafés, stores, lumber warehouses, charcoal kilns, grocery stories, all opened lazily.

Activity, however, increased as the sun rose higher. Passers-by became more numerous, with their odd mixture of colours and clothing, and from here and there strange faces appeared, visages still crinkled with sleep, like bees coming out of a hive.

Life was beginning anew.

Bom-Crioulo slowed down his pace, reducing his speed, calculating the distance, on his way to the house. He could already see it in the distance. It was the same as before, exactly the same, with its antiquated colonial appearance, with its two front windows, and up above, on top, on the roof, a sort of attic, hidden, buried, almost hanging suspended.

He felt an indescribable emotion, a sort of nostalgia, like something penetrating his very soul — the pain of an ancient act of ingratitude, almost extinguished now. Yes, it was the pain of ingratitude. It was there that he had joined his body and his life to the cabin-boy's with the confidence of young lovers; it was there that he had spent the best days of his life; it was there that he had learned to love and cherish.

And he mumbled to himself, swimming in the river of his reminiscences, borne by the unbroken current of his tender memories: "That house! That house!"

He recalled clearly, precisely, the day when he and the boy returned from the long sea-voyage and went there together, to that attic room, where days before a Portuguese immigrant had died of yellow fever. Ah! he had it all in his head still. Well he remembered: the first night, Aleixo's shy reluctance, the scene with the candle. It was all engraved in his memory — every detail!

His eyes filled with tears; he couldn't see properly. It was better not to think of it.

Bom-Crioulo felt more deserted now than ever; the cabin-boy's disdain for him hurt him more deeply than ever — the deliberate, calculated, wilful disdain with which Aleixo was destroying him, was making mock of him without suffering any consequences. "Aha, so that's the way things were, eh? Well, he'd pay for it one of these days. People are like glasses of water: they fill up gradually, slowly, till they can't take any more!"

His eyes flashed like two coals, like two torches, behind the damp mist of his tears; his whole body trembled and shook, like an epileptic's: he felt angry, impulsive, upset. He could hardly control himself at the sight of that house, which was like the tomb of all his dreams. He was utterly transformed; he went mad with hatred, foaming with anger, with rage, with jealousy! The very physical appearance of objects, the world around him, the people going by on their way to work, everything his eyes lit upon in that moment of bitterness — even the sun, and the blazing light of day — everything produced in him only an immense fatigue, and called forth from him nothing but blasphemies that poured from a mouth half-opened in an agonised, convulsive smile. He didn't have the courage to look closely at the house, to let his eyes rest on it; he lowered them immediately, numb; "It was right there, right on that very spot!"

Suddenly he started to hear a humming in his ears, like the indistinct buzzing of insects, an uncomfortable, disagreeable, vexing sensation; his legs trembled; he felt he couldn't breathe. It was his nerves, a sudden weakness, an attack, a frenzy, a vague desire to kill, to murder, to see blood. He covered his face with his hands, trembling, and leaned against a lamp-post. He could hardly stand on his own two feet; he had no strength. The hospital had weakened him; it had debilitated him terribly, that "damned hospital." Never again would he set foot there, never again!

The downstairs door of the house was closed; upstairs, one side of a window was open. It looked as though nobody even lived there: a desolate, funereal stillness reigned!

Bom-Crioulo turned on his heels, dazed, not really aware of where he was, his eyes fixed in the distance, up the street, and he started walking slowly, slowly uphill.

Suddenly he recalled: "Ah! The bakery!" He had forgotten. There it was, the same as always, too, the very same, with its big sign out in front, saying "Portuguese Bakery," with its three doors, under a private residence, almost opposite Miz Carolina's house. From in the back came a tempting doughy odour, the appetising smell of hot, newly-baked bread.

He slipped into the store and without more ado addressed the counter clerk, a bright-looking young teenager who, by his mannerisms, must have come from Portugal.

"Could you tell me, please, if a Portuguese lady still lives over there in the house opposite?"

"Miz Carolina?"

"That's the one I mean: plump and pretty."

"Yes, she still lives there, she does!" said the lad, with a spark of malice in his eyes.

"And a boy, a sailor, with blue eyes?"

"He lives there too. They get up late. Lately they've kept the door closed all the time. They usually go out together at night."

"They go out together?"

"They certainly do! I think that kid is a very smart young fellow."

Bom-Crioulo trembled. He was on the point of finding out everything now, from the mouth of the clerk. There couldn't have been a better opportunity, because the owner of the shop was out.

"You wouldn't be making a mistake, would you?" he said, in a tone indicating curiosity, all at once, in an almost pleading voice, his eyes glued on the boy.

And he began to explain, to describe what the Portuguese lady was like and what the sailor looked like: a plump, pretty lady, very elegant, with big eyes, who rents rooms.

"She's the very one, my man!"

"And the boy doesn't even have a beard yet; he's still almost a kid, with blue eyes, very white-skinned, good-looking."

"That's your man," said the clerk. "They went to the theatre last night, to *The Taking of the Bastille*. I know Miz Carolina very well. They even say that she and the boy are lovers."

Almost the same words as Herculano had used! The same story of Aleixo living with a woman! Bom-Crioulo remained motionless, silent, lost in his thoughts. Aleixo living with the Portuguese woman, with Miz Carolina! It was unbelievable, it was an unspeakable insult, a lack of respect for him, it was brazen effrontery, it was scandalous!

"Are you surprised?" asked the boy, staring at the black man, whose eyes now revealed a sad, extraordinary, indescribable expression of melancholy and surprise. "Well, don't be shocked, because it's what everybody says."

And suddenly, interrupting his exposition, he stretched out his arm:

"Look, as if he knew we were talking about him: here the kid comes."

Aleixo was coming out the door, calmly, in his tight-fitting white-and-blue sailor's uniform, with his shirt unbuttoned at the neck and his trousers fitting him exactly right.

Bom-Crioulo had one of those terrible fits that attacked him from time to time. He groaned a hoarse, long, low "ah!", and, light-footed, furious, beside himself with anger, without losing a second, he raced like an arrow into the street. He could see nothing, he could distinguish nothing, in his rage, as if suddenly his sight and his reason had abandoned him. He rushed forward, bumped into the cabin-boy and caught him by the arm.

He was trembling in a terrible nervous crisis; his eyes were red and cold sweat poured from his shining black forehead.

The boy stopped short, surprised.

"Yes, it's me," roared Bom-Crioulo. "It's me in person! You thought it was going to be so easy to take up with that Portuguese woman, didn't you? Look at this face of mine, look at how thin I am, look at what a wreck I am. Look, look!"

And he squeezed the boy roughly, shaking him as if he wanted to knock him down.

"Let's see if you can recognise me, come on! Take a good look at this face of mine!"

The teenager struggled, pale and terrified:

"Let me go!" he cried. "Don't do anything to me or I'll shout!"

"Go ahead then, shout, if you can! Shout, you miserable scum, you brazen pup, you ungrateful cur!"

His voice took on a tone which was both caressing and terrible at the same time; his words came out in an apoplectic, tremulous stammer.

"Go on, shout!"

The boy's face turned red and then pale, he drew back stumblingly, unable to say a word, almost crying, guilt-smitten, his submissive blue eyes reflecting the image of the black man.

"Let me go," he repeated. "I beg you, let me go!"

Passers-by looked at them obliquely and turned to get a better view of them in that position, face to face, close together, mysteriously quarrelling. For Bom-Crioulo did not speak in a loud voice, for everybody to hear. He didn't cause a scandal or raise a fuss; his voice was a cavernous, hysterical growl, a muffled, deep, distant cry.

"Go on, shout, shout for that pig Carolina!"

"Let me go!" the boy continued imploring, trembling and frightened. "Let me go!"

"No, I won't let you go, no I won't, you little bastard, no, I won't let you go, no I won't! I'm Bom-Crioulo, and I'm here before you, and I'm not what you think I am."

"But I haven't done anything! Let me go, it's late!"

The black man's eyes were red and they had a fierce, embittered expression in them. They crossed each other wildly now and then, with a hallucinated, nervous astigmatism.

A man stopped opposite them, to watch; more observers, more spectators, came shortly: a sailor from the Port Authority office, an Italian laden down with a load of sheet iron, a municipal policeman, women, children . . .

There was an immediate struggle to get the best position, a disturbance, an uproar. Whistles shrilled; voices cried "Fight! Fight!" And the crowd there in the middle of the street grew and grew, jostling for a place, pushing, opening up, thrusting forward, forming a wide circle of onlookers around the two sailors, who by now could not be seen.

Trolley-cars stopped. Women came to windows still combing their hair, avid for news. Dogs barked. It was a commotion, a complete disorder. Frightening rumours and vague, half-complete stories circulated. People made up tales of murder, of blood, of someone's head having been smashed in. Every face and every gaze was a question-mark. Soldiers, sailors, policemen came. Doors slammed closed.

Something extraordinary had happened, because, suddenly, the crowd drew back and opened up, in a confused rush.

"Make way! Make way!" shouted soldiers, raising their rifles.

From the second-floor houses, hands pointed downwards.

And Miz Carolina, who had also been drawn to the window by the noise and the voices, saw the cabin-boy lying, bathed in

140

blood, between two ranks of onlookers.

"Dear Lord! My God!"

A cloud obscured her vision, a chill ran through her, and her whole body trembled in horror, pale and motionless.

Many an eye stared up at Miz Carolina's house.

Aleixo was being removed now by two seamen, who carried him like a bale of goods. His complexion was purplish, his body hung slack, his head dangled backwards, his eyes stared fixedly, his mouth was half-open. His dark blue shirt and his white trousers bore great red stains. His neck was completely swaddled in cloth. His arms hung down inert, loose, lifeless, with the laxness of limbs that have been mutilated.

The street was filling up with people at windows, in doorways, on the sidewalks. It was a disorderly, patently obvious curiosity, an irresistible desire to *see*, an irresistible attraction, a need!

Nobody paid any attention to the other combatant, to the black man, who was being marched down the street now, sad and grief-stricken, between two rows of pointed bayonets, in the hot light of morning: everyone wanted to *see* the body, to analyse the scar, to stick his nose in the wound.

But a hearse rolled away, sealed and gloomy, and the crowd of onlookers scattered, scattered, until everything had returned to its customary monotony, to the eternal coming and going of passers-by.